AMIAYA ENTERTAINMENT
Presents

No Regrets

A NOVEL
BY
ANTOINE "INCH" THOMAS

D1445204

Copyright © 2002 by Antoine Thomas
Written by Antoine Thomas for
Amiaya Entertainment
Published by Amiaya Entertainment.
Cover Design by www.AplloPixel.com
Cover Design by Antoine "Inch" Thomas for
Amiaya Entertainment
Printed in the Canada.

ISBN: 0-9745075-1-2
[1. Urban - Fiction. 2 Drama - Fiction. 3 Bronx - Fiction]

This book was written in F.P.C. Lewisburg 2002

<u>DEDICATION!</u>

I would like to take the time out to dedicate this book to the most important people in my life, my family. To my wife Tania who kept me going when times got rough and I wanted to give up, I love you Girl! To my children, Jyamiene and Amiaya, you two precious little ones are my world. I love you guys to death! And to the Creator, the Almighty God, may you continue to bless me and guide me towards a more positive and prosperous future.

Peace!
Antoine

In The Loving Memory Of
Margaret Gay

1943-2004

In The Loving Memory Of
Of
Mary Moore

1948-2004

Preface

Welcome to New York City, a town that never sleeps. The great Big Apple. The year is 1997, and here lies the fate of a young man in a city stricken with poverty and an unbelievable crime rate. It's the home of millions of people and thousands of neighborhoods, but one particular neighborhood stands alone. It's in the Northeast section of the Bronx. It's a public housing development called the Edenwald Houses, where unlike many other housing projects, crime has not dropped, ever! Edenwald was developed in the early 1940s by a wealthy investor who didn't live long enough to see his project fully completed. After the depression, Mr. Eden Wald's Estate was bought out by the Federal government and was eventually turned into a low-income housing project. Edenwald is comprised of two different sized building structures. Some are dual entry, three-story buildings, the others are taller fourteen-story buildings with large lobby entrances and narrow stairwells acting as extra exits or entrances. The housing project is also divided into two sections, the Northside, and the Southside. There are a total of 75 addressed buildings in the Edenwald housing development with large playgrounds on both sides of the project and a small pool on the Southside.

Take a ride with me as we travel through an unforgettable journey of a young man's life. The life of a young hustler who went from lowlife to kingpin, from purchasing drugs on street corners in Manhattan's Washington Heights section to having a cocaine connect so vicious that every shipment is worth over 4 million dollars in street value.

Tone snaps out of his daydream when the judge, a white man in his mid 70s with a full head of white hair and a face full of wrinkles like a Chinese Sharpei strikes his mallet against the polished wood surface on his oak wood bench. "All rise!" demands the voice from the aging Judge John Fargus. The judge presiding over this case, however, showed no emotion during the testimony. It can turn out to be an advantage as well as a disadvantage for the defense. The defense being Anthony Wheeler, also known as Tone on the streets, and his high powered defense team, Mr. David Buckman, Esquire, Mr. Jonathan E. Spiegel, Field Investigator, and Ms. Cynthia Homes, Paralegal. The team took advantage of the judge's nonchalant demeanor and prayed for an acquittal. "Have you reached a verdict yet, Mr. Foreperson?" asked the judge, looking over his wire rimmed glasses.

"Yes, your Honor!" replied Mr. McCoppin, a black heavyset man in his early 50s with salt and pepper hair and pork chop sideburns. The overweight foreman shot to his feet, unfolded a small piece of paper and said, "We The People of the Northern District of New York have reached a verdict. We find the defendant, Mr. Anthony Wheeler, on the count of," but before the verdict is read, take a look inside of this thrilling novel and open your mind to a suspenseful drama you won't be able to put down. Holla at your boy…

Ya Boy Is Back…

WELCOME
to
EDENWALD

CHAPTER ONE

Summer 1986

"Come on!" said Anthony, almost out of breath now from running so fast. Anthony was a few feet in front of his companion waving him on.

"I can't. My chest hurts!" said Slick, tired from the exhausting chase. Slick was hunched over resting his hands on his knees.

Scanning the area, Anthony said, "Where's Dev at? I hope he didn't get caught."

"His skinny ass didn't get caught. That nigga is probably up under a car hiding or something. He never gets caught," said Slick. He too began surveying the area.

"Tone! Slick!" yelled Dev nervously.

"That's him screaming for us now," said Slick looking in the direction of Dev's shouts.

"I know Slick, it sounds like he's over there," said Tone pointing toward a path parallel to the one they just exited.

"We should hide from his ass and scare him when he

walks by," said Slick chuckling.

"Nah, we need to shut his ass up before those security guards know we ran this way."

"That's why I hate stealing shit from Caldor's. They always got security trying to be super heroes," said Slick.

"I know. Word!"

"Dev!" shouted Tone, cupping his hands over his mouth.

"Dev!" continued Slick, following suit using only one hand to navigate his cries.

"Yo! Yo! Where y'all at?" said Dev nervously making his way down a nearby path.

When Slick spotted him, he said, "Over here you fucking turtle," while simultaneously waving him on.

"Why are you always behind us when niggas be chasing us? As tall as you are, and as long as your legs are, you should always be in front of us," said Tone as Dev now approached the area of the woods where he and Slick were hiding.

"Did you drop your joints, or do you still have them?" asked Tone, looking for an indication or sign that Dev had his merchandise hidden on his person.

"I dropped mine. Do you two still have yours?" asked Dev looking at his two friends.

"Yeah, we didn't drop ours. I'll give you two of mine. That way, we'll all have two a piece to sell," said Tone.

"Alright. Good looking Tone. You're always looking out for us yo," said Dev giving his friend a high five.

"We're boys. What do you expect!" The crackling of leaves a few yards away startled the threesome.

"Ayo, who's that walking this way?" asked Slick looking toward a young kid walking in their direction.

As the boy approached the trio, Tone spoke up. "Homeboy, where you from" asked Tone with his arms crossed.

"I'm from Boston Secor Projects," replied the 12 year

old kid nervously.

As soon as it registered that Boston Secor was rival territory, Tone swung and punched the youngster in the face. Slick and Dev joined in and accompanied their best friend as he administered the beating of the 12-year-old boy. After a few minutes of intense pounding, the trio stopped and moved away from the half conscious youth, staring at him as he bled profusely from his nose and mouth.

"Come on y'all, let's get up out of here!" said Dev cautiously as he and Slick began backing up slowly.

Tone wasn't done yet, he scanned the ground until he spotted a small brick. He went for it as his apprehensive friends called out to him.

"Tone, let's go!" yelled Dev sounding spooked.

"Come the fuck on!" continued Slick, clearly agitated.

Holding the boulder high over his head Tone said, "I should kill this Boston Secor ass nigga!" and brought the brick down hard on the kid's head. "Let's go y'all!" he added as he brushed past his two stunned friends.

The threesome began to trot along as Dev decided to speak up, "What the fuck is your problem Tone?" he asked firmly.

Tone kept jogging and said, "Fuck him, he shouldn't have been in our hood," he remained adamant about his decision.

"You could've killed that nigga," continued Dev catching up to his friend.

"But I didn't!" said Tone firmly.

"You're bugged out Tone. You're fucked up in the head," said Dev.

"Let's just forget about the whole shit," said Slick noticing where the conversation was headed.

"Tell your man that then," said Tone looking at Slick, but referring to Dev.

"Dev, you all right?" asked Slick, checking his friend.

"Yeah, I'm alright," said Dev keeping his eyes cut at Tone.

The threesome slowed down and began walking. "Nobody say anything about this!" said Slick looking at his two friends.

"I don't even know what you're talking about," said Tone illustrating his silence by example.

"You already know my mouth is shut," said Dev looking at Slick.

"Now let's get back to the projects and sell these VHS movies to my sister's boyfriend. He wanted eight of them but he'll be alright with the six that we have," said Tone.

The trio walked quickly through the woods and headed back to their housing project. At 12 and 13, they've been making pocket change together for the past two months selling Tone's older sister's boyfriend video cassette recorder tapes for $10 a piece. They'd steal from the Caldor department store 20 minutes from their neighborhood every chance they got.

At 12 years old, Tone was short and stocky. The shorter of his two friends, Tone always claimed the leadership role to make up for him lacking in height. Tone wore his hair low, and always kept it wavy. His caramel tone complimented his handsome features, and his dark brown eyes, thick eyebrows and long eyelashes remind everyone of his older sister Crystal. Tone is also the more aggressive one in his crew. He always causes trouble between his friends and other neighborhood kids and he always makes sure he and his friends are victorious.

Dev on the other hand is the total opposite. Dev is tall and skinny and the more laid back one of the crew. He keeps his hair in a small curly Afro and his light tone gives him the runway model look.

Slick is heavier than both Tone and Dev. Slick is also darker than the two. A few inches taller than Tone and about 50 pounds heavier, he was always looked upon as the quiet body-guard of the crew. When Tone would instigate fights, Slick would be the one putting out the most punishment to their victims. They all went to kindergarten together and have been inseparable ever since.

Reaching their neighborhood, Slick looked around and asked, "Is your sister outside?"

"I don't know. We'll see when we get a little closer," said Tone making his own observation.

"Well there's her boyfriend Bo right there," said Slick pointing to Crystal's boyfriend, a slim brown-skinned dude with a big head and tons of jewelry around his neck, wrists and fingers. Bo was sitting on a parked car in front of his building.

"Bo, what's up," said Tone, giving his brother-in-law a handshake.

"What's up Tone," he replied and gave Tone a quick rub on the head.

"Nothing. My friends and I have some more tapes for you," he said reaching for the movies.

"What do y'all have? And how many do y'all have?" said Bo anxiously.

"We have six of them. All action."

"Let me see. Oh, I see y'all have the Scarface joint," he said looking at the movies. "Matter of fact, give me all of them. How much do you charge for each one again Tone?"

Holding out his hand, Tone said, "Ten dollars."

"Oh yeah, that's right. Hold on," said Bo reaching into his pocket and pulling out a wad of cash. Tone gasped at the sight of so much money and stared in amazement while Bo peeled off six $10 bills. Bo handed Tone the money and grabbed the rest of the movies from Tone as Tone said, "Damn, how much money is that Bo?"

"About a "G" why?"

"What's a "G"?" said Tone squinting his eyes.

"You don't know how much a "G" is?" said Bo laughing.

Crossing his arms, Tone said, "Nah, tell me."

"A "G" is short for a Grand. And a Grand means one thousand dollars."

"That's a thousand dollars right there?" asked Tone pointing at the large bundle of cash with an excited look on his face.

Placing the money back into his pocket, Bo continued with a smile, "Something like that. Maybe more."

"Where did you get all that money from? Do you sell drugs?" asked Tone with an innocent look on his face.

"Ayo shorty, go head. Get up out of here. You're asking too many questions now. Matter of fact, here comes your sister right now," said Bo looking at his girlfriend who was walking in their direction.

"Hi Crystal," said Slick and Dev at the same time.

"What's up y'all. What are y'all up to?" said Crystal giving the boys soft punches to their chests.

"We're with Tone. He's right there," said Slick pointing at Tone who began walking in their direction.

"What's up Crys," said Tone.

Placing her hands at her hips, Crystal said, "What's up Lil brah. Did you bring us anymore movies yet?"

"Yeah, I just gave them to Bo. We were only able to get six this time because we all got chased and Dev dropped the three he had on him."

"How much did Bo give you for them?" she asked.

"Sixty dollars."

"Y'all should be alright now. Y'all can buy all kinds of potato chips and candy with $60."

Tone sighed and said, "But I don't want just $60 anymore. I want a "G"."

"A "G"! Boy, are you out of your damn mind?" said

Crystal raising her voice.

"Nope. I'm just tired of getting chased for 50 and 60 dollars. You can chase me all day for a "G"," said Tone smiling.

Changing the subject, Crystal asked "What's up with Mommy, Tony? Does she have any food in the fridge?"

"Not really. You know her though. She only shops for like two and three days at a time. Do you want me to give her half of my money? Because out of the $60 we just made, Dev gets $20, Slick gets $20 and I get the other $20. Don't worry, I'll give Mommy 10 of my 20," said Tone holding up his money.

"No here! Give her this!" said Crystal pulling out a bunch of 20 dollar bills. "This should be about $300. Tell her to fill that refrigerator up and stop playing."

Tone grabbed the money and said, "Okay. I will. But listen Crys, remember, I'm 12 and a half now. I can't be running around with $20. I need a "G" in my pockets."

"Yeah whatever! I'll talk to you later. Take that up to Mommy right now, and tell her I love her," said Crystal walking away.

"Alright, I love you Crys."

"I love you too Tony."

"Come on y'all, come with me to my house for a minute," said Tone as he, Dev and Slick run to his house. Tone and his friends head up to Tone's house never once leaving the other's side. They can't, and they won't. They've been together for seven years now and nothing can separate them. Nothing!

Instead of Tone's usual agenda of making pocket change, he now has a goal of reaching one grand in his plans. And he'll do whatever it takes to reach it.

CHAPTER TWO

"**B**o, how long will it be before you come upstairs?" asked Crystal standing by the elevator in her building.

"I only got like 10 nickles left. As soon as I'm done I guess. Why, what's up?" said Bo.

"I want to talk to you about something."

Concerned, Bo walked over to Crystal, placed his hand on her stomach and asked, "Is everything alright? Is the baby okay?"

Touching his hand, Crystal said, "Yes, everything's fine. In fact, I just came from the clinic a little while ago and the doctor said I'm five months and that it's a boy and he's healthy. But we'll talk more upstairs. I have to use the bathroom right now. This pregnancy has me peeing all day," said Crystal opening the elevator door.

"Alright, I'll be upstairs in a little while," said Bo.

Crystal, a 5'1" almond complexioned 120-pound tomboy has looks that could kill. She met Bo a year earlier walking from the store with groceries for her mom. Bo spotted her and asked her if she needed help. When she refused, Bo insisted by telling her he'd follow her all the way home screaming "Why are you not home with the kids!" if she didn't give him the privilege of helping. Crystal gave in and Bo played the gentleman role all the way to her house. He even put down the bags at one point to open the door of the building for her. He asked her for her phone number, but she declined saying that they'd see one another on the street again. So Crystal made it her business to walk past Bo's building every day when she went to the store for her mom, knowing that they'd cross paths again. One day during an encounter, Crystal finally gave in and accepted an invitation to a play called "Mama I Wanna Sing." She brought along her younger sister, Antoinette, who always wanted to see the musical. When Bo treated Antoinette like she was one of his own siblings, Crystal went home with Bo that evening and the two have been lovebirds ever since.

"Bo, let me see what tapes my brother brought us," said Crystal to Bo who now entered the bedroom they share at his mother's house.

"Here you go," said Bo passing Crystal four of the tapes.

"I'm going to put Scarface in first. We'll catch the other movies tomorrow or something because Scarface comes in two tapes. This movie is like 4-1/2 hours long," said Bo putting on part one of the two Scarface tapes.

"Bo, I want to ask you something," said Crystal leaning back on their bed rubbing her stomach.

"Oh yeah, you did have something to talk to me about right?" said Bo pulling money from his trouser pockets and placing them on his bureau.

"Yeah, listen! My little brother is a good kid and I don't like him stealing from those department stores all the time. He could get caught and get into trouble. And I don't want him ending up in some youth center until he's 18 over some damn movies."

"So what do you suggest Crystal? He get a job or something?" said Bo leaning up against his dresser.

"He's not going to get a job, he can't. He's too young right now. Even the Summer Youth Program won't accept him until he's 14. That's two years from now." Smiling, she continued, "What I was thinking was if you'd let him help me bag your drugs up for you and you pay him a little something, it'll be safe because he'll be here in the house. Plus he could earn himself some good money," said Crystal putting her palms together like if she were praying. To emphasize her anxiety, Crystal silently mouthed the words, "Please! Please!"

Bo sighed, rubbed his head and said, "Crystal, he's your little brother. Your mom will kill us if she found out I had him doing that."

Crystal pleaded, "She won't know. I'll just tell him to tell her that I'm the one giving him the money. That way, I won't have to worry about him running around in those streets."

"Well he's your brother. It really doesn't matter to me but if your mom finds out, you're the one taking the blame," said Bo giving in.

"No problem Daddy. I got that under control. Now bring your skinny butt over here and let Mommy have some fun," said Crystal pulling Bo closer to her, unzipping his jeans. Bo instantly became erect and the two of them explored each other's deepest love spots even though Crystal was five months pregnant and sticking out like a sore thumb.

"Mommy, I just seen Crystal," said Tone walking into the apartment he shares with his mom and his sister Antoinette.

"Oh yeah, how is she? I hope she's not staying on her feet for very long periods of time. She needs lots of rest. Lots and lots of rest," said Tone's mother resting on her living room sofa.

"Maah, she's going to be alright. You're always worrying," said Tone taking a seat next to her. She rolled her eyes. "Shut up boy!"

"Anyway Mom, she gave me some money to give to you.

Holding out her hand, Mrs. Wheeler said "give it here. And how much is it because you know I'll ask her?" said Mrs. Wheeler trying to bluff her son. Tone was like a grown man in a child's body. He already knew so much about life and about the streets that it scared his mother sometimes.

"She gave me $200 for you. She said to fill up the refrigerator and to stop playing," said Tone as he passed him mother 200 of the 300 dollars his sister gave him.

"You know Dev and Slick were looking for you earlier," said mrs. Wheeler counting the money.

Tone stood up and began walking toward the door.

"I know Mom, I seen them. They're outside waiting for me now," said Tone leaving out the door.

"Stay out of trouble okay, baby? And you know they start shooting when it gets dark so make sure you're indoors," screamed Mrs. Wheeler as her front door closed.

"Alright Mom. And stop worrying," said Tone running down the steps and exiting his building.

CHAPTER THREE

Outside of Tone's building, the trio continued their juvenile antics.

Sitting on the bench, beside his friend, Tone looked at Dev and asked, where's Slick at?

"He's right there talking to Jane," said Dev pointing to Slick who was with Jane talking in the park.

"Did he kiss her yet?" asked Tone, peering at the couple.

"I don't know. You know he's scared."

"He's never going to kiss her. They've been going together since fifth grade."

"I know."

"What about you Dev? What's up with you and Frenchie?" asked Tone looking over at his friend.

"Man, she's been my girlfriend for a few days already. I wrote her a note last week asking her to be my girl and she wrote me back three days ago telling me yes."

"And when are you going to kiss her?" asked Tone returning his gaze to the couple.

Looking over at Tone, Dev said, "Damn, why are you all up in mines Tone?"

"I'm not," said Tone calmly. He shrugged his shoulders.

"What about you? What about you and Antonia?" asked Dev.

"Chill kid! You know I'm the man," said Tone. "She and I watched T.V. together yesterday while her mom was at work. We humped too," he added.

"She let you hump her for real?" asked Dev excitedly.

"Yeah!" said Tone shrugging his shoulders.

"What other girls have you humped Tone?" asked Dev inquisitively.

"A whole lot! Don't sweat mine! You need to be sweating that player right here," said Tone now looking at Slick who was walking towards them.

"Ayo Slick, have you kissed Jane yet?" asked Tone.

"Don't worry about me. Worry about yourself," said Slick looking at Dev.

"What! Who are you getting smart with? I'll suplex your ass again," said Tone standing to his feet.

"You can't suplex me. All you do is Tito Santana's Flying Forearm move because you know if I grab you it's over," said Slick taking a seat beside his two friends.

"Shut up nigga!" said Tone giving Slick a forearm to the back demonstrating a WWF wrestling move. The two begin going at it like two professional wrestlers. They even added sound effects to every move they applied.

"Chill yo! Chill!" said Dev trying to break up the horseplaying his two friends were engaged in.

"What! You want some too!" said Tone excitedly.

"Nah, but here comes Antonia," said Dev looking over Tone's shoulder.

"Where, oh there she is," said Slick finally noticing her as he and Tone fix their clothing.

"Anthony!" shouted Antonia, stopping about 15 feet from where the trio sat.

"You better answer her Anthony," said Dev being funny.

"Shut up nigga! Huh!" said Tone now answering her like a child does their mom.

"Come here stupid!" said Antonia crossing her arms and tapping one of her feet.

"Ooohh!" said Dev and Slick at the same time adding laughter to get Tony mad.

"Shut up y'all! What Dev! Jump! With your skinny ass," said Tone trying to be tough in front of Antonia as he approached her.

"Where's my soda?" asked Antonia.

With a dumb look on his face, Tone said, "What?"

"Where's my soda from yesterday?" She shimmied her neck and rolled her eyes.

"Let me find out you're tricking now," said Dev as he and Slick continue to clown on Tone.

Tone turned around and glared at his two friends.

"Ignore them would you," said Antonia grabbing Tone by his chin so that they were facing one another again.

"I didn't buy you a soda yesterday?" he asked, acting surprised.

"No!"

"Okay. I got you in a minute. I got plenty money. You know that right?" said Tone digging into his pocket.

She stopped him.

"I don't care how much money you have, I just want my soda!" said Antonia looking cute to Tone.

"Hold on! Where are you going to be at when I come back? Because I can go get it for you right now."

"Right here talking to Beissy."

"You're always talking to her. She's stupid."

"Don't say that about my friend Tony!" said Antonia slapping him on his shoulder.

"That ain't my name!" he said.

Rolling her eyes, Antonia said, "It is too! Your names are Anthony, Ant, Tone and Tony, stupid!"

"What kind of soda did you want again?" asked Tone trying to get out of a humiliating situation.

"A Pepsi! And get Beissy and I some sunflower seeds too," she said placing her hands on her hips.

"Alright, I'll be right back."

Tone walked over to his friends and through gritted teeth said "Dev! Slick! Come with me to the store!

"Damn Tone! Let me find out you're spending money already," said Dev laughing.

The trio got up and started their journey to the store.

"Yeah whatever," said Tone. "Oh yeah, I forgot to hit you guys off. My sister gave me some money to give to my mom and my mom gave me like $30. Here, take $10 a piece and I'll keep $10," said Tone peeling a $20 bill from a small wad of 20s in his pocket.

"Good looking Tone. Now I can buy that Bee Bee gun from the hardware store," said Dev.

"Which one? The 357?" asked Slick.

"Yup!"

"He thinks he's Clint Eastwood," said Tone laughing.

"Yeah, and you think you're Bo," said Dev sounding serious.

"Fuck Bo. I'm going to be bigger than he is," said Tone. Dev and Slick remained quiet while walking to the neighborhood store.

Tone made it a priority to be just like Bo. That is, until he went to Bo's house for the first time. After seeing what he saw, he knew he wanted to be larger than Bo.

Jane and Frenchie were sisters. Though they are Puerto Rican, their skin tone is much darker than your average Hispanic. Jane is the older of the two. At 14, she already possesses a body that even 18-year-olds are attracted to. Frenchie is basically a smaller version of her sister. Same shape, same everything. Just a tad bit smaller. Jane looks like her mom while Frenchie in some ways take after their dad. They're both pretty, and they both know it.

Antonia on the other hand, although Spanish as well, is of Honduran descent. She looks more Black American than anything. Her body too is developing fast, but she never shows it off. She stays covered in baggy clothing because right now she's a tomboy. Antonia is 11 years old, but acts very mature. These kids like each other a whole lot. They think its love. They'll see what love is and what it's about if they keep it up.

CHAPTER FOUR

The phone rings. Ring... Ring...Ring...!

"No matter what they take from me, they can't take away my dig-na-tee/because the grea..."

"Is that the phone Mom?" asked Antoinette as she mimics Whitney Houston's Greatest Love of All hit song.

"I think it is darling. Do you want me to get it?" asked Mrs. Wheeler, Anthony and Antoinette's mom.

"No, I got it," said Antoinette picking up the phone.

"Hello Netty!" said Crystal who calls Antoinette Netty for short. Crystal was lying in bed rubbing her stomach, a habit she became accustomed to.

Antoinette took a seat in her kitchen and said, "What's up Crys?"

"Nothing!"

"How's the baby?" asked Antoinette twisting the phone wire with her fingers.

"He's growing."

"Are you having a boy?" asked Antoinette excitedly.

"Yup! He's going to be big too."

"What are you going to name him?"

"After his father! What did you think?" said Crystal raising her voice.

Scrunching up her face, Antoinette replied, "Okay. Damn! You don't have to get all snotty."

"Shut up! Do you still have my earrings?" said Crystal chewing her gum loudly.

Sucking her teeth, Antoinette asked, "Where else are they going to be?"

"Where's your brother?" asked Crystal changing the subject.

"In jail again, where you think."

"Not Eugene."

"Oh Joe, I think he's selling drugs somewhere out of town. He's been going to Washington D.C. a lot and coming back with lots of new things."

"Oh yeah, does Mommy know?"

"I think she knows. She just hasn't said anything yet."

"So where's Anthony?" asked Crystal.

"I think he's outside."

"If you see him, tell him to come over to Bo's house because I have to talk to him."

"So when are you coming over so I can see how fat my wobbly walking sister is getting?" asked Antoinette laughing.

"I might come over later. My feet are killing me right now. They're swollen at the ankles so I'm trying not to walk on them too much. I'm trying to rest up now."

"Mommy's always screaming, 'make sure Crystal's not on her feet! That baby this! That baby that!'" said Antoinette causing them both to laugh.

"Netty, have you spoken to Juanita?"

"Oh yeah, we talked last night. She asked about you. I told her you have a new boyfriend and that you two were doing well together."

"Oh yeah, what did she say?" asked Crystal as a huge smile spread across her face.

"She said she'll pray for you. As usual," said Antoinette laughing.

"Did you tell her I was pregnant?"

"Yeah."

"What did she say?"

"She was excited. You know she loves you so much."

"Did you give her my number?"

"I think Mommy gave it to her. She'll probably call you on the weekend. The rates are lower then."

"Well alright, when you see Anthony, don't forget to tell him I said to come over. And keep working those vocal chords of yours girl. You know we need us an R & B singer in the house." They both laughed as they hung up from one another.

Mrs. Sonia Wheeler, Anthony's mom, is a 44-year-old, old-fashioned woman. She has a very light complexion and a thick build. Standing at only 5'2", she has a voice that commands the respect of anyone in her presence. She's hardworking and single. She became a widow in 1977 when her husband was killed in a drug deal gone bad on 144th Street and 8th Avenue in Harlem. A few weeks after the funeral, she moved with her six children to the Bronx. They've been living in the Edenwald Houses now for about nine years and have made the best of what they've been able to come across. Tone is the youngest of all six. His oldest brother, Eugene, is always in and out of prison for committing petty crimes. His oldest sister, Juanita, moved up to Syracuse, New York and joined the fire department. She broke barriers becoming the first female firefighter in Syracuse's history, and she made history because she's a black woman. Crystal, the next one down the line enjoys living Ghetto Fabulous. She dates a drug dealer and deals drugs herself. She is extremely kindhearted and the entire neighborhood loves her. Her younger brother Joe is an up and coming hustler. He tries to outdo his older sister by making moves in other states. Currently, he's in Washington, D.C. feeling out their drug polluted blocks. Antoinette, Netty if you let Crystal tell it, is all about school, working and singing. She's very free spirited and loves her family very much. She's an aspiring singer, and hopefully one day she'll get her big break and tour overseas with the man of her dreams. Until then, she practices day in and day out singing along with old Jazz and Rhythm and Blues tunes. The Wheeler's are your average family. Anthony on the other hand is just not your average kid.

CHAPTER FIVE

"Anthony, Crystal said go over to Bo's house. And let me know when you're going, I want you to drop something off to her for me," said Antoinette.

"Are you paying me?" asked Tone, always about making a dollar.

"I only have one dollar."

"Give it to me, I'm going over there now."

"Hold on!" Antoinette retrieved a dollar bill from her stash and grabbed Crystal's earrings. "Here," she said, handing him the earrings and the dollar. "Don't lose that!" she yelled as Tone talked away.

"I won't. I'm not stupid."

Tone got to Bo's house and knocked on the door.

"Who is it?" yelled Crystal.

"It's me!" replied Tone.

"Hold on!"

After unlocking the door, Crystal invited Tone inside.

"Damn Crystal, this house is nice," said Tone scanning

the well kept apartment.

"I know, Bo hooked it up for his mom," said Crystal doing the same.

"Come in the room!" she added. Walking back to her bedroom.

"Whose room is this?" asked Tone entering one of two bedrooms.

"Bo and I share this room." Said Crystal plopping down on her bed.

"What's that Crystal?" asked Tone pointing to a mirror with what appeared to be a razor blade and a white powdery substance lying atop of it.

"It's cocaine!" said Crystal retrieving the mirror.

"Is that what Bo be selling?"

"Yeah, he makes a whole lot of money too."

"Do you be selling it too?"

"No! I just bag it up for him. I put it in these little bottles right here for him," said Crystal pointing to a small pile of empty cocaine vials and their tops.

"Let me do one!" said Tone.

"Do what?" said Crystal looking at Tone like he was crazy.

Pointing at the paraphernalia, Tone said, "Let me see if I can put that stuff in the bottle."

"Here, come over here. And be careful. You don't want to drop that mirror. That's like $500 worth of stuff right there," said Crystal motioning with her hands.

Tone sat on a crate and placed the mirror on his lap full of cocaine. He took the Gem Star razor and scraped some of the white powder into the bottle almost filling it, but leaving just enough room for the top. He then put the top into the bottle making the perfect $5 vial of cocaine. Tone then proceeded to wipe his irritated nose with his hand.

"Don't do that! Are you crazy? Don't ever, not ever

once let me catch you putting that stuff near your nose!" shouted Crystal violently tugging on his arm.

"I'm not. I was just wiping my nose," said Tone.

"Use your sleeve next time! I know you don't want to end up like Joo Joo did," Joo Joo was one of Crystal's cracked-out neighborhood friends.

Tone pondered for a moment then asked, "Is that what happened to her? She sniffed this stuff and went crazy?"

"Well, she actually smoked Angel Dust. That's what made her bug out like that."

"What's angel dust?" asked Tone. Tone was very inquisitive. He wanted to know anything and everything about the streets.

"Nothing boy, never mind the angel dust. This is what I wanted to talk to you about. Are you still trying to make some money?"

"All day, Crys," said Tone passing her the mirror.

"Well listen. I spoke to Bo and he said you can help me sometimes bottling up his cocaine and every ounce you bottle up, he'll pay you $50."

"How much is one ounce? What do it look like 'cause I'm not trying to be bagging up all day for no $50. Mess around and have me looking like Pookie and them on New Jack City," said Tone referring to a recent movie pertaining to Harlem's drug scene.

"This is an ounce right here!" said Crystal showing Tone one of several bags containing 28 grams of cocaine.

"That's it? Only that? For $50? Bet!" said Tone excitedly.

"Yeah, but you must make up at least 150 bottles. That'll give him $750. He breaks you off your $50 and keeps the rest."

"When do I begin?" asked Tone thirsty for some money now.

Shrugging her shoulders, Crystal replied, "Right now if you want to."

"Yeah, I want to! When do I get my $50? As soon as I'm finished?" he asked.

"No! As soon as he's finished."

"What do you mean, as soon as he's finished?"

"When all the drugs are finished and gone, depending on how many ounces you bag up, you get paid then."

"So I can bag up more than one if I want to?"

"If you can handle more than one."

Accepting the offer, Tone said, "Give me one for now. Give me a half an hour, and I'll let you know. I should be done by then."

Crystal handed Tone everything he needed to carry out his task. Two hours later, Tone was still at work, on his third ounce.

"Crystal, put the other tape in! The first Scarface is finished," called out Tone. "Crystal! Crystal!" he shouted.

"Huh!" said Crystal jumping up from her nap.

"I didn't even realize that you fell asleep. But yo, the tape stopped. Put part two in now," he said looking over at Crystal who was snuggled under her blanket.

"You still didn't finish that one yet?"

"I been finished that first one. I'm on my third one now. It's like 187 bottles in that one. And like 181 in that one. Either or but one is like 181 and one is 187. They all look good too," said Tone pointing to two zip lock bags on the floor full of coke bottles.

"Yeah, they do look good. I didn't know you were going to do any more," she said picking up the product and examining his work.

"Why, he's not going to pay me or something?" said Tone stopping in his tracks.

"No, he'll pay you. I just didn't think you'd grasp on to

it so quickly."

"I told you Crys, I'm 12 ½, almost 13 now. And after seeing Bo with that "G", I want one myself now. So I figure, I bag up 20 ounces, then I'll be the "G-Man'," said Tone sounding as serious as cancer.

"Yeah, you'll be the 'G-Man' alright, tired and numb as a motherfucker. After you finish that third one, chill out. Just do two or three each day because we don't need all of that stuff bottled up and just laying around here all day. I'll let Bo know how many you did. I'll call you tomorrow and let you know when you can come back and do some more. For now, finish that up and let me know when you're done."

Crystal headed for the bathroom to take a shower. When she was done, she came back and saw Tone glued to the tube mesmerized by Tony Montana, all the coke he had, and all the guys he was shooting.

She called out his name. "Anthony!"

"Huh." He didn't budge.

"Are you done?"

"Yeah, it's right there. The third one. That one came to like 176," he said never taking his eyes off the television screen.

"Okay, get up out of here. Bo should be upstairs any minute now."

"Anthony! Anthony!" she continued.

"Huh." He still wouldn't move.

"Get out already!"

"Okay. Okay. I'm going," said Tone getting out of his seat.

"We need to expand Crystal," said Tone mimicking the movie star. "New Jork, L.A., Chicago."

"Shut up Tony. That's a damn movie. Now get your butt out of here," she said spanking him softly on his backside.

Tone left the apartment thinking to himself, "Who do I trust? Me! That's who! I made me! Joo Hasa! Joo pig flying sideways! Fuck Frank! Jeah! Fuck Frank! Fuck Bo too! This is Tony's time."

CHAPTER SIX

One week later …

"Ayo Tone, are we going to Caldor's today?" asked Slick as the trio sat in front of Tone's building.

"Nah, I'm not going back to Caldor's anymore," replied Tone.

"Why not?" asked Dev.

"Because."

"Because what?" he insisted.

He wanted to know why Tone declined.

"Because I got me a job now."

Said Tone folding his arms and giving his friends a smirk.

"With who? Where?" asked Slick.

"With the mob nigga!" said Tone changing his smirk to a smile.

"Yeah, right! Come on, let's go to Caldor. We need some money Tone. Plus there's nothing else to do," said Dev.

Trying to reason with his friend.

"I'm for real," said Tone.

"What! About the mob?" asked Dev.

"No, my job nigga! I've been helping out my sister bag stuff up for Bo and they pay me for it."

"Bagging up what?" asked Slick.

"Drugs?" asked Dev.

"Yup!"

"What kind?" asked Dev.

"How much are they paying you?" inquired Slick.

"I be putting coke in little bottles that I guess Bo resells for $5 a piece. They usually give me an ounce at a time to do."

"How much does an ounce weigh?" asked Dev.

"Twenty-eight grams. Anyway, I have to make about 150 to 180 bottles off of every ounce."

"How do you like, you know, do it and stuff?" asked Slick.

"Yeah, what do you use? Gloves and masks?" asked Dev.

"No nigga! I just use a mirror and a razor. I be having everything organized. I make one pile of empty bottles, one pile of the tops, and I use an empty VCR tape case to put the finished product in. It's simple, and it's making me a rich boy," laughed Tone.

"How much are you making?" asked Dev.

"Fifty dollars."

"Damn, he must have you bagging up all night," said Dev.

"Nah, I get $50 for each ounce that I bottle up. And I be bottling up three ounces in two hours."

"How many have you bottled up already?" asked Slick.

"Three."

"So that's $150 you got on stash already nigga?" asked Dev.

"Nah, he hasn't paid me yet. I'm waiting now. Crystal told me he'll pay me once everything is sold."

"You mean when he re's up again?" asked Dev.

"Yup!"

"So when is that going to be?" asked Slick.

"I don't know you fat mafucka! Stop asking so many questions! Fuck is you the police?" said Tone leaning in Slick's face.

"What nigga!" said Slick demonstrating a wrestling punch to Tone's head.

"Come on then!" said Tone as he raked Slick across his eyes while stomping his feet for the sound effect. The two went at it for about five minutes.

"Ayo Slick! Yo Slick!" screamed Dev.

"What Dev?" said Slick bringing his behavior to a halt.

"Stop playing and come on!"

"Where are we going?" he asked still holding onto Tone's shirt.

"We're still going to Caldor's! Tone hasn't gotten paid yet and my stomach is in my back."

"Nigga, your stomach be in your back even when you're full, you Kareem Abdul Jabar looking ass nigga!" said Tone as Slick released the grip he had on him.

"Come here you fucking midget!" said Dev now chasing Tone. Tone tried to stop, moved again and dodge Dev.

"Ayo, that nigga's head is mad big Dev. Just grab his helmet," said Slick laughing himself to the ground. Dev begins to laugh with him and can't take it so he stops chasing Tone.

"Your mother's head is mad big! Fuck are you talking about!" said Tone a short distance away resting his palms on his knees in a bent over position. Tone's a Gemini and has a habit of flipping moods at the drop of a dime.

"Yo Dev," whispered Slick. "Go that way and we'll block his big head ass in."

"I see y'all scheming. Never would y'all catch Mrs. Wheeler's son sleeping. Especially Fat Albert." Tone ran off towards Bo's building.

"Fuck it Dev, we'll catch his bowling ball head ass later."

"Do you still want to go to Caldor Slick?" asked Dev.

"Yeah, do you?"

"Yeah!"

"Come on!" said Slick as the duo began their journey to the department store.

Tone got to the front of Bo's building and the place was deserted. A guy who looked like a drug addict exited the building.

"Hey, lil man, you working?" asked the guy.

"Nah," said Tone.

"You know who got something?"

"I might know somebody, why, don't nobody have anything or something?"

"Hell nah, little man. Everybody's looking. I guess 5-O must've been through and scared everybody off," said the guy looking around.

"Who's 5-O'?"

"The police! Who you think?" said the man.

"Oh yeah, that's right!"

"Aye, does he have something?" said a female drug addict to the guy that Tone was conversing with.

"I don't know. That's what I'm trying to find out myself," responded the guy.

"Do you have anything shorty? He's cute too. I bet you he'll love me to suck on that little dick of his," said the lady smiling.

Tone blushed and said, "Hold up! I'm going to see right now. I'll be right back."

Tone ran up to Bo's house only to find Crystal half

asleep. Anxious and not thinking, Tone entered Bo's house without knocking. "Crys. Crys!" he yelled heading into her bedroom.

"What!" she answered leaning up in her bed. Tone entered her bedroom excitedly and said, "There's people outside waiting for stuff. Where's Bo?"

"He's not outside?" she asked. Crystal was tired and still half asleep. "Nope! Nobody's outside. I think 5-O rolled through and cleared everybody out," said Tone hoping he used the correct term.

"Would you like to do it? Because I'm not selling shit. I can't run in this condition."

"Yeah, give me some!" he said rubbing his hands together and blowing on them like if they were cold.

"They're in there," said Crystal pointing to her bottom drawer. Tone kneeled down and tugged on Crystals bottom drawer.

"All of these?" asked Tone pulling out a bag full of vials.

"Yeah, but come here! Take ten at a time. And be careful!" she said handing Tone ten of the miniature bottles.

"Alright!" said Tone grabbing ten vials and running back downstairs.

Reaching the lobby, Tone screamed out, "Ayo! Ayo!" to a hungry pack of drug addicts standing around.

"Hey! Hey! Shorty brought us something!" said the drug-addicted guy to a mob of cocaine users and crackheads. They all rush little Tony.

"Ayo, hold up! Hold the fuck up!" said Tone with hardly any base in his voice. "Get the fuck in line, and one at a time. Somebody stand outside and watch out for 5-O too," he said emphasizing his demands with his hands.

"I see you learn real quick lil man," said the guy.

"Nigga, my name ain't lil man; it's Tone. Big Tone to

you!" said Tone looking the man up and down.

"Alright Big Tone. Big Giant, Humongous Tone," said the fiend laughing. "What do you have Tone, dimes or nickels?"

"I got dimes!" said Tone not knowing how much they cost but he knew not to sell it cheap and take a loss.

"Let me see one!" said the lady.

"Me too! Let me see one too!" said another lady.

"Damn, these look like nickels."

"Yup! These are nickels."

"Nickels?" said Tone as he looked into his own hands. "Well fuck it then, take y'all $5 asses somewhere else then! Get the fuck up out of here!"

After realizing they had no other choice, the group purchased all ten vials for $10 a piece. Tone counted up $98. "One of y'all shorted me! Fucking crackheads!" he yelled to the group as they hurried away to take their ride to cloud nine.

"Hey little man," said a lady who remained behind.

"What's up! What do you need?'

"Two! I want two of them!"

"Hold on, I'll be right back," said Tone as he dashed back upstairs to Bo's house on the third floor of the 14-story building. He opened the door and found Crystal eating some rewarmed Chinese food.

"Do you want some?" asked Crystal. Offering Tone some of her food.

"Yeah, but hold up. I still got money to make."

"Well where's the $40 at?"

"What $40?"

"I gave you ten nickels and whoever sells a nickel for Bo, he gives them $1 off of each vial."

"Oh word! Hold up then! Let me make this next sale first."

"Do you need any more?"

"Yeah!"

"How many?"

"Give me like five more."

"That'll be $60 when you're done," Crystal said firmly.

"Alright, I got you."

Tone dashed back downstairs after Crystal gave him five more vials. He looked around outside but didn't see anyone. He entered the lobby and saw the lady holding the elevator door partially open.

"Right here little man!" she yelled softly.

"How many did you want again?" Asked Tone walking toward the lady and searching his palm for a full bottle.

"Hold on little man. Let's talk on the elevator."

They got on the elevator and the lady who now looked like one of Tone's classmate's mom also looked good and healthy.

"Little man, I want two of them, but I don't have any money," she begged.

"Well, this is not my stuff. I can't give you any for free," he said placing the vials into his pocket.

"I don't want it for free. Come here!" she said calling him with her finger.

"What!" Tone approached her slowly.

The woman dropped to her knees and unzipped Tone's shorts to find his penis already hard.

"Damn little man, your thing is so big!" she said lying.

"For real? I knew it!" said Tone excitedly.

The woman put her lips around Tone's manhood and began sucking. "Mmmm! Slurp! Mmmmm! Slurp!

"Hold up, I have to pee," he said pulling his rod from her mouth.

"Well wait until we get to the 14th floor."

He agreed. "Alright!"

"Here we are," she said smiling. All she really wanted was her drugs.

Tone got off of the elevator, ran up to the roof and urinated.

"Here I go little man," said the lady. As he dashed back down half a flight of steps, Tone unzipped his shorts again, but this time the lady pulled his shorts to his ankles. She took him into her mouth and gently moved her head back and forth. After about a minute, Tone said, "Hold up, I have to pee again."

Sucking her teeth, the drug addict asked, "Why do you keep on peeing?"

"I don't know, it tickles," he said chuckling.

"Well go ahead, I'll fix that next time," she said as he ran back onto the roof and this time, only a drop came out of his hard weener. He returned and saw her lying on her back with one pant leg off along with her panties.

Surprised, he asked, "What are you doing Miss?"

"Come here! Put your thing in me!"

"What!"

"Just come here!"

"Don't I need a condom?" he asked shyly.

"Why, do you have something?"

"No!"

"So why do you need a condom?" she said smiling.

"Never mind, come on!"

Tone walked over to the woman and climbed on top of her. He put his thing in side of her and startled the lady by saying, "Ooh!" He gasped.

"Huh!"

"Nothing!" Said Tone.

"Are you okay in there?" she asked.

"Mm Hmm!"

"Keep going then!"

Tone continued "Ooh! Ooh! Ooh! Ooh! Ooh! Ooh! Ooh! Ooh! Ooh!" He moaned softly.

"Slow down little man!"

"Ooh! Ooh! Ooh! Ooh! Oooohhh! Oooohhh!" he said emptying himself inside the woman.

"Why are you laughing, Miss?" he asked.

"Nothing. No reason. Are you finished?" she asked smiling.

"Yeah!"

"Are you sure?" she continued laughing now.

As he crawled off of her, bashfully, he asked, "Yeah! Did you feel me inside of you Miss?"

She smiled. "Yeah, I felt you alright."

"Here, take two of these then," said Tone reaching into his shorts pocket while pulling them up.

"Thank you little man. Can I call you big man now?" Asked the lady, smiling as she got herself dressed.

"Yeah, but don't tell anyone, okay?"

"Your secret is safe with me," she said placing her right hand on her chest.

Tone ran down the 11 flights of stairs to reach the third floor. He entered Bo's apartment again and this time realized that Bo was also home.

"Crystal!" he shouted.

"Yeah Tony," she answered from her bedroom.

"I'm here! Do you want me to come into the room?" he asked standing at the front door.

"Yeah, you can come back here."

"Come on young'en!" Screamed Bo.

Tone entered the room. "Here y'all, $75!" He offered Crystal the money.

"I Told you all he wanted was $60," said Crystal looking up at Bo.

"I know, but I just wanted you two to know that I'm good with this," said Tone.

"Let me see," said Bo taking the money from Tone and counting it.

He handed the money back to Tone. "Yo, you keep that! I owe you $75 more."

"Good looking." said Tone.

"Crystal, did you save me some food?" Asked Tone.

"Boy, you took too long. My tummy was still hungry so I ate it all. Anyway, you have your own money now. Go and buy yourself some."

"Alright."

Tone left the apartment.

Bo sat down on the bed beside Crystal. "Yo, your little brother is serious about this money,"

"I told you. You thought I was playing." Said Crystal with a serious look on her face.

"He's just so short. Your whole family is short though. He has a big ass head too," said Bo laughing.

Pouting she said, "Leave my brother alone!"

"I'm just playing. I got love for your brother too. He'll grow into his head one day and turn out to be a handsome young man," said Bo trying to be nice.

"Come and rub your son for a little while," said Crystal, pointing to her stomach for some loving attention.

CHAPTER SEVEN

Three days later …

"**A**nthony! Anthony!" Mrs. Wheeler was yelling in the direction of Tone's bedroom. "Anthony!"

"Huh!" he replied half asleep.

"Your friend is on the phone!"

"Huh!"

"Dev is on the phone!"

"Alright! One second!" Tone got out of his bed and grabbed the phone.

"Hello!" he said.

"Yo!" replied Dev.

"What's up!"

"Were you sleeping?"

"Hell yeah nigga! I'm doing big things now so I gotta get my beauty sleep," said Tone stretching and yawning.

"Get the fuck up then!" yelled Dev directly into the phone trying to get Tone mad. "Nah, what time are you coming outside today?" he added.

"Give me like 45 minutes."

"Alright! I'm a go and snatch up Slick and we'll meet you in front of your building."

"Ah-ight!"

"I'm out!"

"Peace!" said Tone hanging up the phone. He got up and made his way to the bathroom. He got ready to urinate and noticed something. "Damn! What the fuck is my thing doing stuck to my boxers?" He thought to himself. He peeled his penis away from his boxers and noticed a gooey substance at the tip of his member. "Oooww!" he shouted as he released a string of urine. "What the!" he said quietly to himself before trying to urinate again. "Sss, oooww! Shit!"

Are you alright in there boy?" asked Mrs. Wheeler standing right outside the bathroom door.

"Mom, come in here for a minute!" he pleaded.

"What is it? What's the matter?" she asked entering the restroom.

"Mommy, my thing hurts when I pee."

"What! Let me see!" said Mrs. Wheeler removing Tone's sore penis from his boxers. She examined it and said, "Boy, you got gonorrhea! She took a step back, looked down at Tone and asked, "who the hell have you been with?"

"Nobody!" said Tone nervously.

"You have! You just don't get no shit like this by yourself. Now who've you been with so we can notify her parents?"

"Nobody!" he maintained as he pulled his underwear back up to his waist.

"You have! And it better not have been no goddamn crackhead boy. You can get sick out there! Are you crazy?" said Mrs. Wheeler even hyper now.

"Maaah! I was with some little girl in the park a couple of days ago. We did it in the grass," said Tone wanting to tell the truth at first until his mom began yelling and scared him half to death.

Standing with her hands crossed she asked, "Well where the hell is she?"

"I don't know Mom. She ran out of the park when we finished."

Mrs. Wheeler knew Tone was lying. All parents know when the child they've raised from a newborn to young adult is not telling the truth. A parent can instantly pick up the habits and behaviors of their child. The parents can detect it.

Mrs. Wheeler decided not to press Tone anymore and instead said, "Get dressed. We're going to the doctor!"

When they got outside, Tone immediately noticed Slick and Dev.

"Slick! Dev!"

"Yo!" they said together.

"I'll be right back. My mom wants me to go somewhere with her real quick."

"Where are you going?" asked Slick.

"I don't know! With her somewhere," said Tone lying.

"Alright! We'll be right here when you get back."

At the Clinic!

"Wheeler! Anthony Wheeler!" shouted a nurse from a room that read 'Clinic' on its door.

"Right here Miss! We're right here!" said Mrs. Wheeler as she grabbed Tone and walked him into the room.

"Hello ma'am, how are you?" asked the nurse. She was a short spanish lady in her mid-30s with long curly hair.

"I'm fine, thank you," replied Mrs. Wheeler exploiting her fake smile.

"Okay, ma'am. I'll need him to come sit over here on this bed so I can take a look."

"Take your ass over there!" said Mrs. Wheeler in her

killing me softly voice.

"Sit right up here. And what's your name young man?" asked the nurse as she prepared herself for the examination.

"Anthony," said Tone hopping up on the examination table.

"How old are you Anthony?"

"I'm 13," he said lying.

"He's 12 darling," said Mrs. Wheeler giving Tone a mean look. Tone sucked his teeth.

"Okay, Anthony, I just have to take a look here, so lay back okay?" Tone laid back and let the nurse examine his penis.

"Well Anthony, looks like someone didn't use protection. Do you know what a condom is Anthony?" Asked the nurse as she changed her surgical gloves.

"Yes ma'am," he said shyly.

"Do you know how to use one?" she asked retrieving the necessary tools needed to perform the full examination.

"Yes ma'am," said Tone looking at the nurse strangely now.

"Well why didn't you use one?"

Scrunching up his face he answered, "Because I ain't have one."

"Anthony! You have to be careful. Mistakes can and will happen and sometimes we can't fix them."

"I know!"

"Lay your head back for a second. And this might hurt a little bit," said the nurse as she inserted a Q-tip like instrument into the head of Anthony's penis.

"Oooww!" he yelled.

"Is everything alright behind that curtain?" asked a concerned Mrs. Wheeler.

"Yes ma'am. I just needed a sample of the puss so I could test it," said the nurse as she walked with the Q-tip in one hand and a small clear disk-like container in the other. A few moments later, she returned and explained her diagnosis. "Mrs. Wheeler, your son has an STD. The sexually transmitted disease is called gonorrhea. Gonorrhea is a contagious sexually transmitted inflammation of the genital tract caused by bacterium. This infection isn't fatal, but he's fortunate that you noticed it early on. Any untreated infection can cause problems to other organs in the body and we don't want that."

"Will you prescribe some medication for him?"

"Yes. I'll first inject him with a liquid dosage of penicillin; several milligrams at once will begin the healing process. Then he'll get a ten-day supply of the pills. If the bacteria remains or returns at anytime, please notify a doctor as soon as possible. He should be okay in a few days, but have him finish the entire prescription to make sure we attacked the germs. My advice would be for you to communicate more with your son. He's young and at his age, he's curious. Also, keep some condoms at home. Not to encourage him, but obviously he is sexually active and it's better to be safe than to be sorry."

"Yes, I know. I understand. Thank you."

"Anthony! I have to give you a shot now and then we'll be done."

"I hate needles!" he said grabbing his arm.

"It'll be quick sweetie. You want to feel better don't you?" she asked squirting liquid from the tip of the huge needle she retrieved from her tool tray.

"Yes!" he said coyly.

"Okay. Pull your boxers down and bend over."

Confused, he replied, "What!"

"No Anthony, it's going into your cheek."

"Oh!" said Tone positioning himself for the needle.

"Here goes!" said the nurse now puncturing Tone's butt cheek.

"Oooowww! What the fuck!" he screamed.

"You see, wasn't that quick?" said the nurse with a

smile as fake as a three dollar bill.

"Ma, let's go!" said Tone walking out of the examination room after pulling his pants back up gently so as to not tap his sore swollen penis head.

"Mrs. Wheeler, if you don't mind, you'll have to sign something and I also have to give you his prescription."

"Okay. Anthony! Wait for me out front." After signing the necessary documents, Mrs. Wheeler and Tone exited the hospital's emergency room and headed home. Tone was embarrassed so he remained quiet. He and his mom hopped inside of a $1 cab and headed back home to the projects. He knows now that he must protect himself whenever he has sex with anyone. And never ever have sex with a crackhead again.

CHAPTER EIGHT

December, 1988 - two years later …

"Excuse me sir, but how much is this Honda Elite 150 Deluxe?" asked Tone to a mechanic at a local motorcycle shop called Webster's 'Scooters', located on Webster Avenue and Gunhill Road in the Bronx.

"That's a new one there young man. Isn't she beautiful?" said the man pointing at the motor bike.

"She sure is," said Tone wearing a large gold rope chain, a lion's head filled with large diamonds and rubies as a pendant, a matching nugget watch and bracelet, one on either hand, a large nugget 4-finger ring, and a custom made Gucci sweat suit.

"I tagged her at $3,200. Give me $2,900 and she's yours," said the man tapping the seat on the brand new bike.

"What about tags?" asked Tone.

"Now that's another story," said the mechanic.

Pulling out a large bundle of cash, Tone said, "I got $4,000 right now."

"Well then sonny, I think maybe I can find something

around here that looks like a tag and registers like a tag," said the bike mechanic looking like the devil himself.

After giving her a test ride, Tone purchased a matching Sky Blue helmet and rode off with his brand new 1988 Honda Elite motor scooter and headed straight for the highway. Tone rode until his tank flashed empty. He barely made it to a nearby gas station. After a two-hour ride, he filled her up and headed for the projects. In a little over two years, Tone went from bottling up coke for Bo to distributing his own crack cocaine right beside him as friendly competition. Bo is extra large now and no one is actually competition for him. All of the other hustlers in the neighborhood get happy when Bo runs out of product. This makes it easier for them to get rid of their own product which is of less quality.

Tone was back in his neighborhood.

"Beep, beep! Beep, beep!" called Tone with his mouth.

"Is something wrong with your horn because my name ain't Beep Beep!" said Tenequa, a 15-year-old church girl from Edenwald. Tenequa is a month younger than Tone and she's every 15-year-old's dream girl. However, Tenequa has a complex because she wears glasses.

"Well I didn't know your name, and beep beep sounds much clearer than me yelling out 'excuse me'," said Tone sitting on his new bike.

"Don't they call you Tone?" she asked resting her weight on one leg.

"Who's they?" asked Tone blushing.

"Everybody!" said Tenequa waving her arms.

"Well you never called me Tone. In fact, you never called me at all," said Tone smiling.

Folding her arms she replied, "That's because I don't know you boy!"

"Oh, so now my name is boy?"

Tenequa sucked her teeth.

"What's your name by the way?" asked Tone.

Switching her weight to her other leg, she answered, "Tenequa, but everyone in my family calls me Nequa."

"Where do you live Nequa?"

"On the Northside."

"Oh, you mean the Softside!"

"Whatever! Don't you go with Antonia?" she asked rolling her eyes.

"Nah! We used to talk, but she went back home to her country to visit for one year."

"Oh yeah, I heard she was an immigrant," said Tenequa sarcastically.

"She's not an immigrant. She was born here in this country. Both of her parents were born in Honduras, but they have citizenship here in the United States."

"Oh! So who is your girlfriend now?"

"You, if you want to be," said Tone smiling.

"Me! Boy are you crazy! My mother would kill me if she even caught me talking to you. She thinks you're a hoodlum."

"Why would she think that?"

"It's obvious Tone," said Tenequa rolling her eyes.

"I'm no hoodlum. I'm just a gangsta on some thug shit getting this money. Now! Will you be my girlfriend or not?" he said folding his arms.

"You don't even know me Tony."

"You're right, but I have a gun and if you ever tried to play me, that'll be your ass. Nah, I'm just kidding. Only kidding. I seen your eyes light up like the fourth of July. Nah, but I've seen you around. You and your mom and y'all's 1,000 brothers and sisters squeezing up in that van going to church a few times," said Tone laughing. "Why do y'all go to church everyday anyway?"

"We don't stupid! We just go like four times a week. We

have Bible studies. We feed the homeless. We have choir practice and we attend regular service. You need to take your butt to church."

"I'm not ready to go to church."

"Well when will you be ready?"

Fed up, Tone replied, "When I'm ready, that's when! So are you my girlfriend or not?"

"Umm hmm," she mumbled.

"So can I have a kiss?" he asked poking out his lips and closing his eyes.

She screamed, "No stupid!"

"Why not?" he asked returning his face to a relaxed position.

"I'm not kissing you!" she said folding her arms.

"Forget it then. We're boyfriend and girlfriend that don't kiss. It's all good. Well now that you're my never kissing me girlfriend, I'll be on my way to handle some business," said Tone starting the engine on his motor scooter.

Sucking her teeth, she asked, "What, to sell drugs?"

"No! Don't worry about it! And what size do you wear?" he asked.

"Why?"

"What size shoe do you wear Tenequa?"

Looking at her feet, she replied, "A five, why? You plan on buying me some new sneakers?"

"Well Christmas is right around the corner, you never know!" he said smiling.

Tone revved the throttle on his new bike and rode off with a girlfriend under his belt. Tenequa ran home to tell her sisters and friends who her new boyfriend was.

A few minutes later…

Tone decided to stop off at the store first. He got off his bike and entered the eatery. "Boom!" Tone heard a loud crash and ran out of the neighborhood pizza shop.

"Ayo, who the fuck dropped my bike on the ground!" shouted an angry Tone. He looked around and saw a familiar face.

"Me you punk!" said another 15-year-old who lived in the projects as well.

"Oh, Leslie Boyd! You think you're tough because it's like 30 of y'all. Nobody told your mom to be a doorknob and to give everyone a turn. I should beat your ass since you're all by yourself," said Tone mocking Lenny's name to make it sound feminine.

"Yo Dee! Malik! Sean! Lindsay! Gene!" Five of Lenny Boyd's brothers filed out of the game room adjacent to the pizza shop. "Look what we have here. We finally got your little fronting ass," said Dee, second to the oldest of the Boyd brothers.

"Let me fight him!" said Malik, a year older than 15-year-old Lenny.

"Nah Malik, Lenny is going to fight him," said Dee.

"Man fuck all y'all! All y'all can suck my dick!" said Tone picking up his bike. Lenny and Malik attacked Tone. They knocked him to the ground, and when he realized he couldn't take the both of them, he balled himself up and the two played soccer with his big head and tiny body.

"Hey, hey!" yelled Iggy, the Italian pizza shop owner as he rushed outside to aide poor Tone. Iggy pulled Lenny and Malik off Tone. When Tone got up, all he said was, "Y'all fucking with me, then y'all fucking with the best!" he put on his helmet and rode off.

Ten minutes later …

"Here comes Tone now!" said Dev sitting beside Slick on the bench.

"I see he wasn't playing. He did go back and get that

shit," said Slick referring to Tone's Honda scooter.

Tone pulled up and parked his bike.

"Damn Tone, you crashed already?" asked Dev.

"Tone, are you okay?" asked Slick.

Tone didn't acknowledge his two best friends. He just took off his helmet and walked toward his building.

"Leave him alone then, with his funny acting ass," said Slick.

"He thinks he's all that cause he got a bullshit ass scooter," adds Dev.

"What! What the fuck you say nigga!" said Tone now approaching his friends. "Say it in my face!" Tone was standing in front of the duo now.

"Be easy Tone!" said Dev noticing that Tone looked a little disheveled. "Tone, what happened to your forehead? Your shit has a knot on it," he added.

"You and fat ass want to play all the time. This is not a joking matter. The Boyds jumped me down at the pizza shop. It's on now! I'm not taking any losses, ever!" said Tone walking to his building.

"I see the Boyds gave his little ass the blows," said Slick laughing.

Elbowing his buddy softly, Dev said, "Chill Slick! Tone is serious right now. You're playing and you know he's going to do something crazy about it. That nigga already thinks he's Tony Montana, and we definitely have to be there for him.

9:30 p.m. That evening...

"There goes Tone right there," said Slick still sitting on the benches.

"Tone! Tone!" said Dev.

"What!" said Tone stopping to acknowledge his buddies.

Concerned, Dev asked, "Where are you going?"

"I'll be right back!" said Tone getting on his bike dressed in an Army green camouflage fatigue suit.

"I told you he was up to something," said Dev.

"Tone is crazy, but he's not stupid," said Slick.

"Watch what I tell you. Watch!"

Five minutes later...

While Slick and Dev were engaged in their street antics, from a distance, they heard muffled gunshots.

"Pop, pop, pop, pop! Pop, pop!"

"Yo, do you hear that shit Slick?" asked Dev looking around.

"Pop, pop, pop," continued the shots.

"Hell yeah! Niggas is shooting on the Northside."

"It stopped!" said Dev quieting down and searching with his eyes for more gun shots.

"Probably somebody just testing their guns again," said Slick.

A few seconds later, Dev said, "Probably. And there goes the sirens. Another false alarm I bet," he said as sirens blare from a distance.

Two minutes later Dev looked up and said,

"Ayo, doesn't that look like an ambulance that just went into the Northside drive?"

"Hell yeah!" said Slick.

"Let's check it out!"

"Come on!"

They Duo ran to the Northside and saw a crowd of people gathered around a circle full of police officers. In a double-parked police car sat Dee Boyd with blood stains on his shirt near his shoulder talking to an officer.

"Aaah! It hurts! Get me to a hospital!" moaned Dee Boyd to the officer driving the vehicle.

"Calm down, you're in shock. A second ambulance is

on its way," said the officer.

"This one is losing blood. I see four visible holes. One in his neck, and three in his torso. I need I.V. I need an I.V. now!" shouted one of the paramedics attending to Malik Boyd.

"Did anyone see anything?" asked a uniformed officer to a group of people who gathered at the scene.

"Yeah, I seen everything," said Malik's brother.

"Who are you? What's your name kid?" asked the officer.

"My name is Lenny Boyd. These guys are my brothers," said Lenny Boyd pointing to his two brothers who had been shot.

"Well what exactly is it that you saw," asked the officer retrieving a notepad from his back pocket.

"We were all right here in front of my building…"

"Who's we?" asked the officer cutting him off.

"Me, my brother Sean, my other brother Lindsay, my other brother Gene and my two brothers Dee and Malik, the ones that just got shot."

"Okay, so what happened?"

"You see those bushes right there?" said Lenny pointing to an untrimmed bush in front of his building.

"Yeah."

"So the bushes began to rattle and shake. So we were all sitting on the bench right here," said Lenny pointing to a bench located less than 15 feet from the bushes, "and the bushes kept rattling. So I'm high, and I'm tripping."

"You're high young man?" asked the officer. Surprised, he let the witness continue.

"Yeah," answered Lenny.

"Off what?'

"Trees!"

"What, marijuana?"

"Yes."

"Hold on a minute. Rogers. Come here a minute," said the uniformed officer to another uniformed officer. He whispered something in his ear, then returned to continue questioning young Lenny. "So you're high young man? Let's get that clear one more time."

"Yes, and anyway, the bushes started to rattle. Then it stopped. Then it started rattling again, then it stops again. So my brothers Dee and Malik move close to the gate to get a closer look because we all thought it was two cats fighting or something. Next thing you know, it was like the 4th of July out here. Fire everywhere. I mean it looked like somebody was firing from a blow torch because a light was steady coming from the bushes, but it was like bolts of lightning or something. Then we heard loud ass firecracker sounds and my two brothers drop to the floor like the dead men do on T.V. They start screaming and what not, 'My neck, my back, my neck and my back. My shoulder.' It was scary, but it was funny too. I mean officer, imagine your front bushes rattling, you investigate and Rambo's in there with a machine gun. It was crazy officer."

"Well do you have any idea who would want to shoot you guys?"

"Yeah," said Lenny smiling. "You police dudes," he said laughing now.

"Listen here young man, we're going to need you to come with us for further questioning."

"Okay," said Lenny accompanying the officers.

The first ambulance rushed Malik to the hospital at about 10:02 p.m. The second one rushed Dee at approximately 10:06 p.m. People began clearing out slowly and Slick and Dev eased their way off without being seen. They walked back to their side of the projects, the Southside, with ear to ear grins on their faces.

"I told you!" is all Dev could say.

Dee and Malik survived, but the rumor was out that

Tone shot them with an Uzi. No one could prove it so the police refused to pursue it. Dee and Malik began attending church services regularly after they were released from the hospital. All of the brothers saw Tone on Christmas Day when Tone was on their side of the projects bringing Tenequa her Christmas gifts. Malik, permanently in a wheel chair, simply yelled over to the two lovebirds, "Stay away from the devil Tenequa! Stay away from the devil!"

Tenequa heard the rumor and she loved the attention she was getting from her friends about her dating young Tone. The boy with the itchy trigger finger.

In the months to come, Tone had been in a number of altercations. In one instance, he thought he was being tailed by someone from a rival neighborhood. His instincts had paid off because after cornering the guy and stripping him down to his underwear, the guy told him how he was paid to find out where Tone hung out and also to see if he could locate where he lived as well.

"What nigga done lost his mind and sent you on a suicide mission?" said Tone, holding a .357 revolver halfway down the terrified guy's throat with the barrel of the gun pressing down on the guys tongue, he did his best trying to explain.

"I lont low his lame," said the guy nervously.

"Well you better tell me something," said Tone cocking back the hammer and shoving the gun further into the guys mouth.

"Aw-wight, Aw-wight. It was Calwin and lem from 213th.

Tone pulled the gun from the dudes mouth and said "who?"

The guy said "Calvin, that nigga been sweating you ever since you bought that scooter."

Tone put the gun back into the dudes mouth and continued speaking.

"Oh yeah! I ain't never liked that frail mafucka since he pulled up in front of my school fronting in his lil Jeep Wrangler. You're lucky I don't feel like killing nobody today. Get the fuck out of here!" said Tone. The guy looked up at Tone, Tone looked down at him and withdrew the gun from the guys mouth once again.

The guy turned and began to run. Tone then shot him in the buttocks which made him laugh as the guy squealed in agonizing pain. That night, Tone rode through Calvin's block on a stolen Kawasaki Ninja and let off 36 rounds from his Mac. II semi-automatic Uzi, hitting two innocent bystanders. Though he didn't hit his intended target, Calvin did get the message. After that, Tone didn't have any problems with Calvin or anyone else in the surrounding neighborhoods.

CHAPTER NINE

March 1, 1989 …

The local police were notified by the principal of junior high school, John Philip Sousa, 142, that a young man had plans to shoot all of his classmates in school. The tip came from a young Guyanese student who liked Tone, but kept getting rejected by him because to him, she wasn't popular, and he was. The police searched Tone's coat and retrieved a 380 semi-automatic handgun. Tone was subsequently arrested and charged with possession of a firearm in the third degree and disorderly conduct for trying to push the cops out of his way to give him running space. Though Tone was a juvenile, it was his fourth case, all felonies. Tone wasn't going to shoot any of his classmates, the gun was for some guys who kept coming around Tone's school looking for him. In the past year and a half, Tone was arrested for grand larceny when he got caught in a brand new 190 E Mercedes Benz he took from a crackhead who owed him money. The crackhead never showed up at court, but the state picked up the case. After realizing he could go to jail for felonious antics, Tone calmed down and hit the drug scene hard. Eleven months after his grand larceny charge, he was arrested for possession, with intent to distribute, 360 vials of crack cocaine, an A class felony. Two days after that, he was arrested again by the same undercover detectives, this time with 400 vials of crack cocaine, a package he took four hours bottling up for himself. Due to his age, all three times he'd been arrested, the police had to release him to the custody of his mom, who was always crying, worrying about her baby. Today, however, a more serious crime had been committed. With three open cases, the judge had more than enough reason to commit Anthony to the Spofford Juvenile Correctional Center located in the South Bronx. Miraculously, at Anthony's third court date, exactly 15 days from his arrest, a plea deal was made. If Tone stayed out of trouble and remained in school for the next two years, his sentence would be suspended in exchange for two years' probation. Tone walked out of the Bronx Family Division Court saying to himself, "They should have never let me go. All they did was give me a green card like they did with Tony Montana at the INS facility he was held at."

On the other hand, the courts had other plans. The courts knew that young Tone had a pattern of arrests which meant a history of crime was associated with it. They figured, if Tone could just last long enough to reach his 16th birthday, then he'd be considered an adult, and with his experience, even more dangerous. Lo and behold, they were right.

May 12, 1989. In front of Tone's building...

"Tony! Tony!", shouted a crying friend of Crystal and Bo.

"What! What's up Rah?" Rah used to be a member of Bo's crew but after numerous allegations of him trying to sleep with Crystal, Bo cut him off.

"Something happened!" he said crying harder.

"Something like what? Is Crystal okay?" asked Tone.

"No!" Said Rah shaking his head with disgust.

"What! What's going on Rah? Talk to me," insisted Tone.

"I don't know Tone! I don't know!" said Rah bowing his head.

"Where are they? What hospital?" said Tone standing up from the bench.

"They're not in the hospital. They're bodies are still in the house." Said Rah sadly. Tone looked in the sky and couldn't help but lose the strength in his legs. He knew whatever happened to his sister was bad. He dropped to his knees, clinched his two fists and screamed louder than he ever screamed in his entire life, "Nooo!"

Crystal, her boyfriend Bo and their bodyguard were killed at their home the night before. Word on the street was that it was a robbery gone bad, that someone entered the house with intentions of taking any money or drugs that were found in the apartment. According to police, however, the perpetrators were more than likely acquaintances of the deceased because 'Gangsta', a red nosed pit bull that Bo had specifically trained to guard them and to attack anyone unfamiliar to him was found roaming the crime scene without his harness. Sources said Bo only removed Gangsta's harness when everyone was in for the night and when he was on patrol. Crystal and Bo left behind two beautiful children, two-year-old Bo, Jr. and 5-month-old Tianna, their daughter, who was found clinging to her mother's lifeless body. Seventeen month old Bo Jr. was visiting with his grandmother, Bo's mom, on the night of his parents execution which is probably what saved his live. Had he been present the killers may have assumed that he could possibly have identified them which would have given the shooters more than enough reason to assault him as well. Forensic experts determined that the killer or killers were already in the house when Bo and his bodyguard were caught off guard and ambushed. Bo was brought into his bathroom and pistol whipped before being shot once in the head at close range and placed in his bathtub. The bodyguard had apparently given the gunmen a struggle before being shot once in the face and twice in the chest because in the living room, where he died, lamps were knocked down and the carpet had marks as if someone were digging their feet deep into them. After Bo and his bodyguard were killed, Crystal came home only to discover her dead fiancée and friend and was then ambushed by the killers who never realized that she had her daughter in her arms. Crime scene officers said in an attempt to save Tianna's life, Crystal gave her own. Though there were the fatal bullets that ripped through her head and shoulder, the hand that wasn't holding Tianna had a bullet hole going right through the center of it as if she were trying to block the bullets that killed her.

The perpetrators responsible for Crystal, Bo and their friend's death were never apprehended. No clues, no suspects, and no clear motive, although it was apparent, were found, arrested or established, in that order respectively, and from that day on Tone wasn't the same.

At Crystal's funeral, about 150 family members and friends attended. Crackheads, coke heads and heroine addicts who Crystal would give free hits to on the second and the sixteenth of every month, when everyone was broke, even showed up to show love. The eulogy was given by Pastor Randy Green, a family man who came to New York three years earlier from the southern part of Virginia to practice and share the word with a larger audience.

"Would anyone like to share anything with us expressing their feelings toward this young lady who left us at the tender age of 24 years young, to be in the blessed company of our Dear Lord?" asked Pastor Green.

Tone got up from between his mom and sisters and

approached the podium. Everyone was surprised.

"I'd like to share something with everyone in regards to my sister sir, if you don't mind," he said climbing a stool and adjusting the microphone to his height.

"No, go ahead. Take your time young man," said the pastor moving out of Tone's way.

Tapping the mic for a sound check, Tone cleared his throat and began to speak. "Hello everyone. As most of you all know, Crystal was my favorite sister." Choking back tears, he continued. "Regardless of what her lifestyle may have been, she was always a very generous, caring and loving person. She'll definitely be missed by us all, but I personally lost the closest thing to me." Pausing again, he wiped his eyes then proceeded. "Please, everyone bear with me as I read this poem I wrote the day after my sister died. It's called, 'I Won't Forget You,' and here it goes."

Tone pulled the poem from his front pocket, unfolded it and rested it on the podium. He cleared his throat and before he could say anything, his sister Antoinette broke out in a loud holler and began screaming, "Nooo! Whyyy! Why my sister! Noooo! Nooo!" Eugene and Joe, her two older brothers assisted Antoinette and calmed her down. No matter how hard Tone was, losing his sister made him realize that he had a soft spot. Seeing his next closest sibling crying like a baby, a tear that he never thought existed in him, flowed smoothly down his right cheek. After everything was calm, he began reciting his poem.

"I won't forget you, even though you're gone,

Even though the life you lived most would say was wrong.

Still I won't forget you, your smile or that lovely face,

Till God brings us back together, no one can take your place.

You were my Sunshine, whenever it would rain,

And now that my sun has disappeared, all I feel is pain.

I won't forget you, because you are a part of my crying
soul,

The warmth in my heart, a heart that many said was
cold.

I still can't believe you're not here by my side,

When your life was taken away, a part of me also died.

Even though you're gone, always I will miss you,

Through life, till my last day on earth, Crystal I won't
forget you."

At that point, the entire audience broke down and cried.
Tone walked off the podium and sat between his mother and
Antoinette. "Don't worry Mom, somebody will pay for what
happened to Crystal. I promise you they will," said Tone mean-
ing everything he said.

CHAPTER TEN

May 11, 1990...

On the eve of Crystal and Bo's one-year memorial, Tone sat alone in front of his mother's building contemplating how to celebrate the following day.

"Tony! What's up," said Black, a 16-year-old neighborhood trouble maker. Black was 5'9", 140 pounds, tall, dark skinned and skinny. Black seemed to have appeared out of nowhere.

"Ain't shit. What's up with you Black? I haven't seen you around in a while," said Tone shaking hands with the guy.

"I know, I just came home from Riker's Island," said Black taking a seat near his friend.

"What did you do time for?" asked Tone.

Looking out at the park, Black thought to himself for a moment, then began to speak. "A stolen car. I know somebody told on me because I got snatched up before I even made it back to the car. It probably was Little Moe and them because earlier that day, I caught them trying to thief my shit and I beat Little

Moe's ass. What's up with you though. I see you're over here in a daze," added Black looking down at Tone.

Playing with his hands, Tone proceeded to speak. "Nah, I'm just thinking about what I'm going to do tomorrow for my sister's memorial. Tomorrow makes one year that she's been dead. What are you doing in this neck of the woods Black?" he asked, turning and looking his associate in the eyes.

"My mother just moved in your building."

"My building?" said Tone straightening up in his seat.

"Not actually your building, but the one connected to it. My window is right there in the front," said Black pointing to a third floor window that has a view of the entire neighborhood.

"Oh, okay," said Tone looking at the window.

"Tone," said Black.

Tone answered without raising his head. "What."

"Did they ever find out who did that to your sister?"

"Nah. Why?" said Tone now looking at Black.

"Because, you know, people are saying that you yourself are crazy enough to do something like that to your own sister."

"What!" Tone never heard anything like that before and whether or not it was a rumor, it was a statement that snapped Tone into a twilight zone. Tone pulled out his nickel-plated 45 and began hitting Black upside his head with it. When Black fell to the ground, Tone continued smacking Black all over his head and face with the gun. At the same time, a squad car from the PSA Housing Authority was doing a routine patrol and spotted Tone beating Black senseless.

The police car jumped the curb and raced to Black's aid. "Freeze! Don't move!" said the cops as they jumped out of their car and approached Tone cautiously.

Tone never heard a word. All he felt was the sting from the billy club that struck his head, and then he went out. Tone tried to get an insanity plea, but the judge saw his face too many times before. The court's plan had finally taken effect. Anthony Wheeler was sentenced to three years in a correctional facility in upstate Coxsackie, New York. Slick and Dev remained in the streets hustling and occasionally visiting Tone. Tenequa wrote Anthony on three occasions and stopped for unknown reasons. Antonia, on the other hand, returned from her native Honduras to find five letters addressed from Tone on her bureau. She began writing Tone and for the two-and-a-half years that she kept in touch with him, she wrote every week. Six months before his release, Antonia wrote Tone telling him that she was accepted into a nursing school for interns. She had plans of one day opening her own pharmacy and she had to get all the credits she could in that field. Tone had a few months of good time taken from him, but by him acquiring his G.E.D., attending college courses from professors teaching at the prison who were teachers at SAGE, Junior College of Albany, as well as obtaining a certificate, certifying him to be an electrician's helper, he was released after spending almost 40 months in prison.

CHAPTER ELEVEN

August 31, 1993. Anthony just turned 19 four months ago,
becoming a man in prison.

"Move over Slick! You know you're still fat as hell," said Tone causing Dev to start laughing. Tone's two best friends, Slick and Dev picked him up at the Port Authority bus station in downtown Manhattan, New York City.

"Damn, you got big kid," said Dev looking over his shoulder from behind the wheel of his Mazda van.

"Tone, are you trying to see your P.O. first or do you want to go shopping first?" asked Slick turning around to face Tone who was resting in the back seat of the vehicle. Dev adjusted the rear view mirror, looked at Tone and said, "Yeah because that tight ass sweat suit you have on makes you look like you have on Speedos," said Dev laughing.

"I'm not on parole. I maxed out. Now we can definitely get me out of this spandex suit, but what's up with some food?" said Tone leaning up and placing his arms on both the driver and passenger seats.

"What do you want, McDonald's?" asked Dev.

"Hell no! That's McDevil's if you ask me. I don't eat red meat anymore. I only eat fish and poultry," replied Tone.

"Oh yeah, that's right, you's a Muslim now," said Slick causing the trio to laugh.

"Aye Tone, look we understand you're just coming home and everything and we respect whatever your decisions are going to be," said Dev driving up the westside highway in his brand new pearl white 1992 MPV, "but we're dealing with the reality of these streets. It's hard out here man. It's really hard. I mean while you were in, I even worked with my uncle at a GMC plant in Jersey City for almost two months. The money was okay, but it wasn't what I wanted. You know what I'm saying? But that's just me. You do you! Slick and I will definitely support you brah, with whatever you do."

"But remember," interrupted Slick, "we'll always have an opening for our brother," he said once again glancing over his shoulder.

Looking at his friends, Tone said, "I appreciate that y'all. I really do. You guys took care of me my entire bid. Y'all wrote me, y'all sent me pictures, y'all even took the time out to come and see me. To be honest, I really don't know what I'm going to do. I never made it my business to form a plan before I got released. Something I should've done. Something everyone in prison should do. Only Allah knows what lies ahead. But I know one thing, I didn't do all of that positive shit in there for nothing. But enough with all that rehabilitation shit. First I'm trying to eat something. Then I'm trying to get out of these tight ass clothes. Then I want to go and see my mom. And before the night is over, I want to be knee deep in somebody's ass."

"Somebody's ass!" said Slick and Dev together trying to be funny.

"Fuck y'all! Nigga I jerked off my whole bid. Never

will I fuck with any of them chump, homo mafucka's. Mrs. Wheeler didn't raise no faggots. Straight gangsta nigga!"

"I thought you was a Muslim? Now you a gangsta?" said Slick still being funny.

"Oh, my bad! You're right, you're absolutely right. Asalaamulaikum!" said Tone now being funny himself.

"Salaikum Salam!" said Slick.

"It's not Salaikum Salam fat boy. It's Walaikum Asalaam."

"Alright. Wah-lay-kum, Ah-sa-laam. Bighead!"

"Ayo, your head doesn't look that big anymore," said Dev.

"It's still big, it's just that he's so backed up that the rest of his body evened out with his head," said Slick laughing.

"Don't make me pull you in the back part of this van and do a Hulk Hogan on you. I still got it kid. And I'm even stronger now," said Tone.

"What you need to do is go and grab you a female and do the Doggy style in some damn hotel. I don't know what the hell you talking all this wrestling shit for. Talk some sex shit nigga," said Slick. "Who are you going to lay up with tonight anyway?" he added.

"I don't know. Tenequa wasn't fucking when I left and Antonia is still away at school."

"Oh Tenequa is definitely fucking. You better believe that. She used to fuck with Reggie's freak ass, hard, last summer. So I know she's fucking," said Dev.

"Fuck it, she owes me a piece of ass anyway. I bought her ass some sneakers and stuff right before I got locked up. Let's do everything else first though."

After making all the necessary stops, Tenequa caught word that Tone was home and met him up in the pizza shop.

At the pizza shop...

"Damn Tenequa, you're looking good!" said Tone.

"You're looking good too," said Tenequa standing around in a spandex flower colored thigh-high summer dress.

"So I hear you're all grown up now. You even traded in those glasses for some contact lenses I see," said Tone looking her up and down.

"Pretty much." She blushed.

"So can I see how much of a woman you are tonight?" Asked Tone in his sexiest voice.

"If you can stop by around 12:30 tonight, I'm all yours," said Tenequa turning to leave.

"Where do you live now? I heard you moved out of the projects," he asked.

"We did, my brother, Montey, kept the apartment in the projects. My mom and us moved to 1985 East 232nd Street. It's a private house. It's actually on 232nd and Laconia. Right at the corner. I have my own apartment on the side of it. It's actually the basement part of the house. Just come over later and I'll have the door unlocked for you and your sexy self."

"Okay, beautiful, I'll be in you later. I mean, I'll be in your house later," said Tone laughing.

"See you."

"Bye."

Jumping back in the van, the trio pulled off. "Okay, Mr. Loverman, let's tour the neighborhood and bring you up to par on a few things like how your man Black had been running around like a killer when you got knocked and all of a sudden wants to hustle downtown in Bronx River Projects when he heard you were coming home," said Slick.

"Fuck that nigga! Fucking faggot! My ass would've beat that attempted murder case on Black if he would've dropped the fucking charges. Now I got a violent felony on my rap sheet because some street punk didn't want to play by street rules. Fucking snitch! You know, in jail, snitches get stitches.

On the streets though, they get put in ditches!" said Tone.

"Be easy son, we don't have to worry about his black ass anymore, he's downtown now," said Dev.

They rode around with Tone until it was time to drop him off at Tenequa's house. That night, Tone and Tenequa made love for the first time together. Tone even performed oral sex on her which was a new experience for him. A week later, Antonia returned home and Tone patched things up with her. Tone heard through a grapevine that Tenequa had several boyfriends on hold. What he didn't know was that he was the only guy who she let have unprotected sex with her. Forty months without vaginal intercourse brought Tone to a climax that naturally ended with one result, that night, Tenequa got pregnant. She didn't realize it until she was four months into her pregnancy. By that time, Anthony and Antonia were once again a couple. Romantically this time.

In the months that passed, Tone put in applications for jobs at numerous business locations. He went everywhere from supermarkets to large business buildings like the Empire State Building and the World Trade Center inquiring about everything from janitorial service to custodial maintenance. Every last one of his encounters were met with unsatisfactory results. After taking a written test for the New York City Transit Authority, then hearing about its 18-month waiting list, Tone finally landed a job sweeping up hair at a local barbershop. This low paying job was very discouraging to Tone and the peer pressure from seeing his friends doing well in the street life, to the feeling of being a grown man and having barely enough to eat with in his pockets caused Tone to relapse and jump head first back into the drug scene. By Christmas of 1993, Tone had three workers and a steady flow of income from the drug game. The money was too overwhelming and Tone found out that he would soon be a father. Plus, Tone loved the streets, so he solidified his position by calling a meeting with the other dealers in his projects at his neighborhood stomping grounds, the Blue Park.

"Check it," said Tone gathered in a circle of the neighborhood's most notorious hoodlums. "I know I've been gone for a minute and I ain't the type of dude who eats out of someone else's plate if I didn't help cook the meal. From what I see, most of y'all are hustling in front of 1132, 1154 and on the avenue in front of the pizza shop. The Blue Park has been dead since I've been gone. I'm back now and I'm going to get the park popping again. I respect the hood so I won't step on nobody's toes. I expect you all to respect the hood as well, so don't step on mine. Do we have an understanding?" asked Tone adjusting the 45 caliber semi-automatic he had tucked in his waist.

A bunch of "um hums," head nods and "yeah, no doubts," told Tone that his message was clear.

"Let's get this money then peoples," said Tone as everyone dispersed and went their separate ways.

CHAPTER TWELVE

1995, The Edenwald Housing Development: The
Southside, Blue Park.

"Ayo Tone, yo Tone!" said Dev to Tone who was in between two cars making a drug transaction to a crackhead.

"Hold up Dev, this dude got mad singles so I have to count all this shit up before he leaves."

"Tone, you haven't finished that package yet?"

"Nah Dev, that shit was some garbage that Poppi and them gave me so I had to recook everything and the 375 grams I originally had, came back to like three hundred and thirty something and fucked me up."

"How much did you bag up off that 300 grams?"

"Only like six thousand and change," said Tone walking over to Dev who was sitting on the bench. "I got like five 20s left and I need all of this money off this pack in order to make this power move I came across."

"What power move are you trying to make without

including me and Slick?"

"Y'all dudes know I'll never make a move without y'all. I'm just trying to see if this shit works out and I'd rather take the loss by myself than feel bad about bringing all of us down if the shit didn't work out," said Tone as he sat beside Dev on the park bench. "What's up with Slick anyway, I haven't seen him all day?" added Tone with a sarcastic look on his face.

"I thought I told you that Slick is having another baby, with Faith this time, and he's been out buying more stuff because this time it's going to be a girl."

"Damn, that's two of everything, two bottles, two shitty diapers, two pairs of Jordan's and two crazy ass baby mamas. I'm glad I only have one little boy by Tenequa's dumb ass and she doesn't even be tripping like Faith and Jane do with Slick."

"That's our man and all that, but son is crazy for having sex with Faith raw like that anyway," said Dev.

"Isn't she a stripper or something?" asked Tone.

"Yeah, and she threw that Harlem coochie on him and he hasn't been the same since. It's like all of his time goes into her and his fat ass is probably tricking all of his money on her too," replied Dev shaking his head.

"What is he reing up with now anyway?"

"I think he's still working with 250 grams. At least that's what he was on when he first started dealing with Shorty. Plus, he hasn't been out here to move shit like he's supposed to."

"Well fuck it, I should be finished this in like another 45 minutes at least, and when all of this is done, I'm a count up all my dough, holla at these peoples, see if I can pull this one thing off, and if I hit, we on. If I miss, then we're still on these benches until the wheels fall off," said Tone as he walked over to another crackhead in a white Hyundai who purchased his last five 20s with a crispy $100 bill. "It's on Dev," he added. "I'm about to go to my house and work my magic and I'll holla at you later," said Tone walking toward his building.

"Okay, then, I'm a go and fuck with this Ruger I just bought from basehead Dave. He gave me two clips and four boxes of shells, Black Talons, for three grams. I whipped it into a half of an ounce. Never would I let a crackhead get over on Mrs. McCray's son," said Dev as he walked down the block to his building.

Tone had grown to be a stocky handsome young man. He stood 5'6", 190 pounds, and still had short wavy hair. Dev was still tall and skinny. Dev grew to stand 6'2" and weighed 180-185 pounds. He too still had good hair but occasionally kept it braided in plaits. Dev was also into motorcycles and learned how to do many tricks on them. He scratched his face once while popping a wheelie during the rain and slipped, damaging the bike, his leg and his left cheek. Slick, on the other hand, had gotten much heavier. Slick now weighed 280 pounds easy and he kept his head shaved so people wouldn't notice him going bald. With Tone and Slick at the young ages of 21 and Dev at 22, it would be pretty embarrassing to have an oldhead look in the hood at only 21. Tone and Dev continued clowning Slick about his obesity, but they have major love for him because he goes hard in the streets for that money, and with beef.

CHAPTER THIRTEEN

Upstairs at Tone's house …

"Anthony! Anthony! Turn that goddamn music down, don't nobody wanna hear that shit all day," screamed Mrs. Wheeler over a Biggie Smalls song called Warning. Tone turned the radio up at first on spite, but then immediately turned it back down in case his mother was really upset about something.

In the privacy of his room, while Biggie Smalls played low in the background and Scarface played silently on his 36" T.V. screen, Tone pulled out a phone number from his pants pocket with a name written above the number reading "The White House." Tone always knew a little Spanish from growing up in the Bronx around Puerto Ricans all day. He was about to make the one phone call that could possibly change his life forever and he felt if he incorporated a little Spanish into his lingo, that it may influence the possibility of making the connection. Tone accidentally stumbled upon the connect by helping a relative of one of the connected cross a busy street in the Bronx.

Once across the street, the elderly Spanish woman thanked young Tone. The entire time, her kingpin son watched from behind the wheel of his luxury sedan that was parked at the corner of the block. He saw how this young man treated his mom with the utmost respect when he didn't even know her. The son then put a tab on Tone and dropped a card off to him one day when Tone was in the pizza shop hanging out. The guy approached Tone and simply said, "Here my friend, call me when you're ready to make your dreams come true." Then he disappeared. Tone felt it was genuine and kept the number.

Tone dialed the number into his credit card thin digital cell phone and on the first ring, a Spanish speaking person answered in a monotone voice. "Si," said the voice.

¿"Qué pasa hermano? Estas tu amigo. La Moreno tu met a la pizzaria," said Tone in his best impression of Tony Montana.

"Si, ¿como esta usted Señor?"

"Muy bien amigo. I'd like to holla and I know bueno business is best done in person. I'm trying to make a good impression for you guys."

"Si hermano, I know what you mean. I know you're serious. It's approximately 2 p.m. Go to the corner of Loring Place and Fordham Road and be by the phone booth with the broken receiver at 2:45 sharp. I'll have some of my people contact you then."

The line went dead. Tone looked at his watch and called a cab. He grabbed his camcorder bag full of money, double checked everything and got ready. When the taxicab beeped to let Tone know it was downstairs, Tone yelled out to his mom that he'd be back later and headed outside. He hopped inside the backseat of the low profile car and as it pulled off, he began praying for his big break like an aspiring rapper would do when handing in his demo to a recording company. Twenty minutes later, the cab pulled up to the corner of Fordham Road and

Jerome Avenue, a few blocks from where Tone was supposed to meet his connect. Being the cautious fellow that he was, he now had enough drop distance for him to scan the area for anything suspicious. With what he expected to take place, anything was liable to happen. Tone might be a gangsta in his own hood, but he's in the big leagues now and playing with a whole other team. After a 15-minute stakeout of the area, Tone began approaching the corner of Loring and Fordham. He neared the phone booth, and as soon as he kindly leaned against the pole, the phone begin ringing. Not knowing whether or not it was a set up, Tone instinctively moved away from the telephone booth and began glancing around at his surroundings while discretely clutching his camcorder bag. Suddenly a black minivan pulled up to the sidewalk. A voice shouted from a cracked tinted window of the van in a heavy Spanish accent, "Walk to the middle of the block behind you to building #4064 Señor. There will be a list of apartment buzzers on a panel in the lobby, press number 9 and wait for further instructions." The minivan immediately pulled off and Tone rushed up the block unaware of what lay ahead of him.

CHAPTER FOURTEEN

Ten blocks down Fordham Road ...

Unbeknownst to Tone's meeting, Slick and Faith were in Jimmy Jazz Sportswear, an urban apparel retail outlet, looking for baby clothes for their unborn.

"Faye, how much are those pink Timberland boots?" asked Slick. "They're hot. My queen'll look nice in them," he added as he held the tiny shoes inches from his face.

"They should be about $30 for infants," said Faye in her heartbreaker voice. Slick always thought Faye had a very sexy and sultry voice. Walking around were a slew of very attractive Spanish girls dressed in skintight jeans and T-shirts assisting customers. A tall thick-thighed Dominican girl asked Slick if he needed any help. She could tell that Slick liked what he saw by the way he was drooling all over her.

Seductively she wiggled her neck and asked, "May I help you sir?"

"Sure, you can help me," replied Slick with a little more base in his voice than usual. "I'd like everything in pink for a newborn baby girl." Slick noticed that Faye was busy trying on items for herself so he took his chance with the store attendant.

"Ayo Shorty," whispered Slick.

"My name is not Shorty. My name is Evelyn and why are you whispering?" she asked resting her weight on her left hip and rolling her eyes.

"Be cool Evelyn, my girl is here with me. I don't need her all up in my business." Evelyn gave Slick a sexy look at first and then flipped out and yelled, "Fuck off jerk!", and quietly walked away. Luckily no one heard the commotion, especially not Faye.

"Faye!" yelled Slick, calling her by the nickname he gave her.

"Huh," she said never looking up.

"I'll be outside getting some air. Get what you have to get but only use the Visa card."

"Okay." Faye being the gold digging, money hungry whore that she was, didn't even realize that Slick had an ulterior motive. To holla at passing women on the street. Slick walked out and almost got knocked down by a guy entering the store who resembled Michael Jordan.

"Passion! Passion! Is that you?" said the Michael Jordan look alike.

"Jayson? Hey baby, how are you doing?" replied an excited Faye. She smiled and stretched out her arms to give Jayson a hug.

"Long time Boo!" He said as he held her in his arms and playfully squeezed her butt.

"Hold on," said Faye looking around for Slick. "Damn Jayson, it's been a while but I see you're still looking good as always," she said looking him up and down as she circled him.

"Thank you! I've been doing real good too. And I've been looking for you. Where have you been? I haven't seen you around in a while. Are you still at Leopard's?" he asked.

"No."

"Well are you still dancing?"

"It depends," said Faye with her killer smile.

"It depends on what?" said Jayson with a smirk on his face. The two engaged in their conversation while Slick was outside chasing women.

"What's up with you, are you still single?" asked Jayson.

"Nah, I have somebody. He's a sucker though. I just fuck with him for the money he's dishing out," said Faye looking at Jayson seductively.

"You still all about that paper, ain't you?"

"Not with you Boo. I promised you something and I never break my promises," said Faye licking her lips and caressing her legs.

"So what's up?" said Jayson.

"You'll have to give me your number because I live with my problem. He's a clown so I'll manage something."

"Here, my pager number and my cell number are on there. Hit me when you're ready," said Jayson passing Faye one of his cards. "And you take care of that fat ass for me," said Jayson squeezing her butt again. "Damn, he must be hitting it right too because it looks like you're getting thicker," he continued.

"I am getting thicker, from sitting around waiting for some dick, if you know what I mean," said Faye referring to her and Slick's lack of sex.

"Alright then, I'll holla," said Jayson leaving the store.

CHAPTER FIFTEEN

At the other end of the block with the deal of a lifetime ...
Tone approached the building and realized that he had to be buzzed up or have a key in order to enter the premises. After about 30 seconds, the door clicked and Tone pulled it open racing inside while cautiously observing everything in his surroundings. He entered the lobby and pressed buzzer number 9. The second door in the lobby clicked and Tone held it open but waited in case someone appeared over the intercom. Suddenly a voice came over and said, "Second floor, numero nueve." Tone dashed upstairs and found door number 9 to the left of the elevator. He knocked on the door.

"Entra!" Said A voice.

Tone entered the apartment carefully while his gangsta kept him calm. A beautiful Spanish woman standing about 5'9", with long black hair, a tan-colored tone, petite build in a cat suit with a face that could double for Jennifer Lopez instructed Tone to have a seat in the living room. The woman quietly strolled toward the rear of the apartment and disappeared into the silence. The living room was small with very little furniture. It had wall-to-wall plush black carpet, a black leather sofa, a black granite coffee table in the center of the living room with a black cordless phone lying at the center of the table. The phone rang and after its tenth ring and no sign of the Spanish lady, Tone decided to answer it himself.

"Hello," said Tone.

"Buenos tardes Señor," said a voice over the phone. "I was beginning to get worried. I didn't think you were going to answer the phone," he continued.

"Oh shit, what's up, I mean ¿qué pasa hermano?" said Tone nervously.

"Calm down hermano. No worry."

"Okay," said Tone regaining his composure.

The man asked Tone his name. "Como se llamo Señor?"

"My name is Tony, why what's up?"

"I feel more comfortable addressing you properly young man. You know, I've been keeping an open mind in regards to you so I want you to tell me what it is that you'd like to accomplish."

Confident, Tone began, "I'm trying to locate the key to the city and open its doors to a prosperous future for myself. I'm trying to have an elite brand of clientele and I want to be able to supply anything to anyone, anywhere at anytime. Basically," said Tone, more confidently now, "I want to do it up Pablo Escobar style."

¿"So you like Pedro Escobar Señor?" asked the guy laughing softly.

"No doubt Poppi."

For the next few moments, everything went silent and Tone knew that the other person on the phone hadn't hung up because he hadn't heard a dial tone. He was hoping that the assumed connect was calculating what he'd charge and what he'd front to young Tony. All of a sudden, the Spanish woman returned to the living room with a piece of paper containing a list of names on it and passed it to Tone. Tone scanned the paper and quickly noticed that some of the names seemed familiar, and some of the names appeared to be foreign. Along side each name were phone numbers. The voice on the other end came back and said, "Did you receive the list?"

"Si Poppi, Yo tengo la papel. ¿Pero, qué es estas?"

"That list is your future Señor. Everyone on that list is a potential client, so it is up to you to fully exercise your ability to do good business. You make your own deals, but what we negotiate is final and never changes under any circumstances unless I say so. And whenever you run out hermano, we'll arrange for you to obtain whatever else it is that you need. ¿Are you okay with that Senor?" asked the Spanish guy.

Firmly, Tone replied, "Yes!"

The note also had some added information. It read:

"Inside the suitcase next to the front door is 75 kilos of pure Fishscale Cocaine and 10 kilos of China White Heroine. I get back $10,000 for every kilo of the coke, and 75 grand for each kilo of the heroine. If you wish to decline this offer, walk out that door right this minute and everything that just happened will not exist anymore. If you agree, you'll walk out that door with the suitcase and a very promising future. On the outside of the suitcase you'll find a detachable suitcase roller. Use it to your advantage. A black minivan will be waiting for you outside to take you to whatever destination. For future advice, relocate your family to a more suitable environment as soon as possible. I don't think the people in your neighborhood will appreciate your new lifestyle within a month or two. Use the money you made on your street corner to work out your relocation situation. If you have any questions, please refer them to Maria, the woman present with you at the moment."

Tone raised his head after reading the note, caught eye contact with Maria and said "Maria, I have no questions at this time,".

The phone line went dead. Tone set up the carrier and rolled the suitcase out to the elevator. He entered it with caution and pressed the button that said lobby. Although given the extra sense of security by the Spanish guy, Tone tapped his own waistband to make sure the neatly tucked 13 shot Dessert Eagle semi-automatic handgun was still in arms reach. Leaving the building, Tone quickly glanced around at anything that may help him remember the location of the building where his life had changed. Upon leaving, Tone noticed a symbol on the gate that reminded him of something. It was an eagle, the same eagle that appears on all American dollars. The tinted minivan's side door slid open and a man resembling Fidel Castor, the president of Cuba, asked Tone, ¿"Where to Señor?"

Either this was all a dream or Tone finally made life imitate art of the movies. "Two hundred twenty-fifth Street, and Laconia Avenue, uptown" said Tone.

After Tone entered the vehicle with the suitcase in tow the minivan slowly pulled off and New York's hottest radio station, Hot 97.1, blared from the minivan's speakers. He heard a song from rapper Nas' album "Illmatic." Ironically, it was the song "Life's a Bitch!", by Nas and rapper AZ. Tone laid back in the soft leather of the minivan's seats and took in the thought of being the next Tony Montana. All he could think about was "Damn, that's damn near 1.5." He also listened to AZ's mesmerizing verse of the AZ, Nas collaboration.

"Visualizing the realisms of life and actuality, fuck who's the baddest a person's status depends on salary/and my mentality is money orientated, I'm destined to live the dream for all my peep's who never made it."

"I'm going to blow for Crystal and Bo," said Tone caught up in his own thoughts.

CHAPTER SIXTEEN

Dev put down his joystick after playing the Super Nintendo computer in a brutal match up of "Mortal Kombat" to answer his home phone. "Hello," he said.

"What's up Boo, you can't call nobody?" asked Frenchie. Frenchie was now Dev's fiancée.

"I've been busy Ma. You know I miss you though. Matter of fact, I did leave messages saying hello and that I missed you and all of that so what are you beefing for?"

"I'm not beefing nigga, I just would like to hear from my man at least once a day, that's all."

"Well what are you doing right now? And what do you have on?" said Dev grabbing his crotch.

"I'm in the tub right now Pa," said Frenchie in her very seductive Spanish accent, "and all I have on is the suds from this bubble bath."

"Oh really! Damn!" Dev began to pant. "Well why don't you grab up B.O.B. and you know," said Dev slyly.

"Are you for real? You want me to grab up B.O.B., my

battery operated boyfriend? That shit is in my room and I'm all wet and relaxed Pa," said Frenchie with a huge smile on her face.

"I'm saying Ma, go head," begged Dev.

"Hold up! I'm all dripping and what not. Hold up though! And your ass better get some lotion or something nigga, you always want me to freak off by myself but you never want to freak off with me. I want to hear you sometimes as well," said Frenchie getting out of the tub and tracking water on the floor to her room.

"Alright whatever. All I need is some saliva though. I go's hard Ma," said Dev.

"You're stupid," she laughed.

"Do you have it yet Ma? My shit is going to get soft already," said Dev stroking himself gently.

"Wait a minute, I don't just be having that thing laying around so people can see it. Wait! Oh, here it is. I have it now Pa. Damn! This shit is all cold and dry," she said examining it. She retrieved the erotic device from a shoebox in her closet.

"Lick it then Ma!" said Dev whispering into the receiver.

Frenchie shot back but then caught herself. "Pa, you lick."

"Yo, yo, yo, yo! Don't even go there! Never am I on some ol' homo shit," said Dev cutting her off.

"I didn't mean it like that Pa. Alright? I'm back in the tub now too honey. Now give me a kiss Pa," said Frenchie entering her bath water with her eyes closed.

Dev paused in mid stroke. "What do you mean, give you a kiss?"

"Damn, at least act like you're here with me. You want to be so thugged out all the damn time."

"Alright Ma, alright!" Dev began kissing Frenchie through the phone and Frenchie started to moan as she inserted the waterproof 8" dildo inside of herself. She slowly made love to herself with B.O.B. and continued to moan just like Dev liked it. Meanwhile, Dev was jerking off like a bat out of hell.

"Pa, Pa, mmm, Pa, Paaahh!" screamed Frenchie.

"What! Wait a minute! Ah, hold up, hold up, hold up, hold, damn!" said Dev reaching his climax.

"Pa, did you cum?" Frenchie sounded disappointed.

"Hell yeah, what the fuck! Ah shit! Damn! Ayo, hold up! Who the hell is calling me at a time like this? Hold on Ma!" Dev clicked over to answer the other line. "Hello!"

"Yo, what's up Dev," asked Tone.

"Oh shit, what's up Tone! What's good?"

"I'm on my way back uptown. I'm going to page you as soon as I hit the projects, and just come through to my house 'cause yo," Dev cut Tone off.

"Hold on for a second Tone. Let me hang up from the other line." Dev clicked over. "Ma, so what's up? Did you cum all in the tub for daddy? Got that coochie juice all in the water for me to drink up?" he said as he wiped his hands clean.

"Yo nigga! You freak ass nigga! This is still Tone! You's a freak ass nigga Dev! For real! You're gone Dev!" said Tone laughing.

"Damn! Pardon self!"

"Ga head nigga, I'll holla in a minute, you ol' Jake Steed ass nigga! Peace!" Tone hung up the phone.

Dev clicked again and got a dial tone. He thought to himself, "Damn! Fuck it, I'm good! I'll holla at her later." He then proceeded to clean himself up.

Tone's crib!

There was a knock at Tone's door.

"Who is it?" yelled Mrs. Wheeler.

Dev looked at the peephole and replied, "Dev."

"Hold on baby, one second," said Mrs. Wheeler as she

opened the door and let Dev inside. "He's in the room darling, go head back there." She muttered.

"Thank you Mrs. Wheeler. And how are you doing today?" he asked being respectful.

She smiled "I'm fine, thank you."

"Alright then." Said Dev brushing past Mrs. Wheeler, heading towards Tone's bedroom.

"Alright."

Dev knocked on Tone's bedroom door. He could hear Tone playing the new DJ Clue CD with the Brooklyn based rap group "Junior Mafia" now showing their skills. Tone opened the door elevating the sound of the music. "I bought wifey a crib and bought the Mafia an arcade/mad games pool tables and candy, a little extra tricking loot be coming in handy/check it, got on some 95' shit, sold the 5 bought the 6, Delvec copped the Lex we was set/Meeno had work all in the projects..."

"Damn that shit is bumping. What's up though," asked Dev. He entered the room, gave his friend the customary hand-shake and sat down on the bed next to him.

"Shit! Ayo Dev, we're on! I did it son! I fucked around and bumped into some Poppi niggaz when I went and purchased them Clue CDs the other day and the guy happened to be a made nigga. Anyway, he gives me his pager number so I called him. Really on some trying to test his work out so that maybe we could have a connect here in the Bronx as opposed to buying from Manhattan, going across that hot ass bridge all the time. Anyway, I fucking paged him and he tells me to come through. His lil spot is on Fordham Road and Loring Place. Anyway, I went through, and he was on some real Scarface movie type shit. He had vans tinted up, creeping up on dudes, and had guys whispering through van windows like "Yo Poppi, go up the block.' Anyway, to make a long story short and a short story even shorter, I went to his spot in some apartment building on Loring Place, and inside was a nice looking Spanish chick. Yo Dev, shorty was bad too. So anyways, I spoke to the dude on the phone at the spot and he had the lady bringing me notes with messages and shit and me and dude talk some more and I wind up with crazy drugs yo. Coke and dope," said Tone excitedly.

"Word up son! What the fuck are we going to do with the dope Tone? And how are we supposed to move all of that shit anyway?" asked Dev.

"You know a lot of dudes on the avenue got dope already. I mean they ain't no killers or nothing like that, but it seems like it's only a few dope fiend niggaz around anyway," added Dev.

"Nah, Poppi gave me customers along with the drugs. He gave me kilos Dev. Crazy drugs, and the customers are probably people buying big weight," said Tone. "Look at this list of names. Some of these people are high up silver spoon ass niggas. Isn't this name like one of our borough reps or some-thing?" asked Tone showing Dev a couple of names on the list.

"Oh hell yeah Tone. So what, you're like a gofer dude or something?" asked Dev seeming confused.

"Hell no, never is Mrs. Wheeler's son somebody's gofer. I just look at it like this. Poppi fronted me some drugs, because never do I work for anybody, and he gave me some customers he don't fuck with. Feel me!"

"No doubt!" said Dev nodding his head.

"So basically, you guys are my peoples so you all are down with me already. We just make all the sales together and blow together, na mean," said Tone smiling.

"So when do shit jump off?" asked Dev anxiously.

"Well I'm not really trying to make it seem like I'm thirsty and jump for dude, so I'm going to holla at Tonia first. I'll probably take her out or something, then get in touch with 'Whipped,' I mean Slick, and then me, you and Slick are going to kick it some more. Then we'll just go hard from there. So for now, just be easy, do you, and I'll more or less hit you when Tonia and I are done, ah-ight!"

"Ah-ight Tone, I'll holla at you later then."

"Ah-ight, peace!"

"Peace!" said Dev as he left Tone's crib. Tone sat back for a minute before calling Tonia. He spun back the CD to his favorite underground song which was playing when Dev walked in. His favorite verse is when 'The Notorious B.I.G.' says ... "Niggaz say I died dead in the streets, nigga, I'm getting high getting head on the beach/chilling, sitting on about half a million, with all my niggaz, all my guns, all my women/next two years I should see about a billion, all from the love of drug dealing..."

"Damn! The next two years," thinks Tone.

CHAPTER SEVENTEEN

Tone calls Tonia at home…

The phone rings …

"Doesn't anyone hear the phone?" yelled Antonia. Tonia dropped the tomboy look after returning from school and is now drop-dead gorgeous. She still has a ghetto appeal to her and will always be classy about herself. She now has long black silky hair and wears grey contact lenses. Her full smile compliments her high cheekbones which give her sort of an Asian look now. She's 135 pounds, mostly buttocks, thighs and calves, and she has a C cup breast size. Her flat stomach makes the front of her thighs look thicker than they really are and her bow legs give her sort of an exotic sexiness.

"I got it!" yelled Michelle, Antonia's younger sister. Michelle is a short and stubby young lady and has a cute face that resembles her sister's. However, Michelle is super duper ghetto. One time she wanted to stay awake in order to study for a test, but didn't have any sugar for some coffee, so she used Kool-Aid to sweeten it.

"Hello!" said Michelle.

"Is Tonia there?" asked Tone. Tone calls Antonia Tonia for short because it sounds like Tone and he always makes her feel like she is his right hand.

"She's here, why?" said Michelle twirling the phone cord with her hands.

"Put her on the phone stupid!" demanded Tone.

"Nigga please! So when you gon hook me up with one of your friends?" she said smiling.

"Chelle, you're only like 14. You need a boy, not a man. Now put your sister on the phone!"

"First of all nigga, I'm 17, and I only mess with men. I ain't got time for little boys out there. The only thing them young niggas got for me is money."

"Well all of my friends have wives and they already know not to fuck with family anyway."

"Yeah whatever! You just don't want them getting open on these thick ass thighs of mine." Before Tone could say something in response to what Michelle just said, Michelle interrupts, "Tonia, the phone! Your fake ass John Gotti husband! And I think y'all got married on the down low too. Ain't no nigga buying no chick a ring that big for nothing. I'm telling Mommy!" said Michelle before she got the phone snatched from her by Tonia.

"Hello," said Tonia.

"Hey, what's up Ma!" said Tone.

"Oh hi Pa, hold on. And take off my damn chain and my earrings! You're always borrowing my shit and that's why my shit is always coming up missing! No! ... Put my shit where you found it! ... Now! Hello!" said Tonia obviously hyped now. "Pa, what's up? I'm tired of her little fat ass touching my things and then when something is missing, she never has anything to do with it, so she says," she added.

"Ma, be easy. Daddy's here," said Tone trying to be sexy.

"I haven't seen you or your lips in like two days Pa. Are you alright?"

"Yeah, I'm good Ma. Check it, I'm trying to see you tonight. We'll go out first, so wear the Coogi dress I bought for you last week. Not the pink one, wear the lavender one, and wear your lavender Gator pumps too."

"Damn, it's like that Pa, what's going on? Let me find out we're celebrating something Pa. What's the occasion? Or is it a secret?" she said blushing.

"Damn Ma, I just love you and I'm feeling you right now, hard for some reason too. Plus like you said, we haven't seen one another in a couple of days and I'm trying to make it up to you."

"Shit, you always duck me for a couple of days here and there. You ain't been taking me out! You must be guilty of something and you're just trying to butter me up in case I find out nigga," said Tonia sounding more suspicious now.

"Well today is kinda special and we have to talk about something important."

"Uh oh, that doesn't sound too cool honey," said Tonia wiping the smile from her face.

"Oh now I'm honey all of a sudden," said Tone with a grin.

"Shut up nigga, you're always honey, as sweet as you are Boo," said Tonia trying to cover up in case she spoiled the moment.

"It's not really anything that deep though Ma. Actually, I'm trying to talk about being closer to you."

"Oh no he didn't. I know my boobie is not proposing to me," said Tonia with a smile on her face a mile wide.

"I told you Ma, like Methodman said, 'You don't need

a ring to be my wife, just be there for me and I'm a make sure we be living in a fucking lap of luxury..." Tone sang.

"What! Forget Meth, I want a damn ring baby."

Laughing, Tone said, "Nah, I'm just playing. You never know though! It might happen real soon too. But I really might be talking about expanding! Feel me!"

"What do you mean expanding? Oh, your ass is trying to go out of town!"

"I'm talking about expanding us Tonia. Our family. You know, little rug rats and shit. The nine month thing. You know, the cravings like peanut butter and pickles and all that," said Tone as they both start laughing.

"Are you for real Pa? You never talked about kids before. You better be ah-ight nigga. And you better not be on your way to do a bid on the low. I always told you to tell me things like that so I can prepare myself for it. You know the stamps and envelopes and all of that jail shit. 'Cause you know I'm not losing you to anything. And if you're talking about something else, when you go, I'm going right along with you. They're going to have to make a bunk bed coffin for the both of us. I ain't playing! And when are we supposed to start working towards this extended family anyway Pa? Tonight?" she asked excitedly.

"Slow down Ma! Just get ready and I'll be through in a lil bit to pick you up. I already made plans for us tonight and everything. Plus, I'd like to show you something."

"Show me what Pa? Tell me, you got me mad open. My thing is wet already just thinking about it all."

"Just get ready stupid. I'll be up there in like an hour, alright. I love you!" said Tone grinning.

"I love you too Pa!" said Tonia. She hung up the phone and started getting ready.

After leaving the Lexus dealer, Tone made arrangements for a suite at the Parker Meridian Hotel in downtown

Manhattan. Rose pedals, champagne, room service, and a seven-minute live tune of Keith Sweat's "Make It Last Forever" was played by a small band using mandolins and violins. Tone went to get his hair cut at "Quran's Barbershop" to help sharpen his look for this special evening.

Tone entered the barbershop and took a seat in the awaiting chair.

"Ayo Tye, where's Quran and Jus?" asked Tone.

"Just chill be, you worrying about the wrong things right now!" said Tye, a brown-skinned slim dude from Brooklyn who moved to the Bronx because dudes in his neighborhood kept vandalizing his barbershop.

"Ayo, I heard about you. Don't push my hairline back son. Word on the streets is that you be zeeking niggaz yo! I heard the last time a kid got his shit cut here, he came back ready to shoot shit up," said Tone joking with Tye.

"Shit, you got me fucked up. A nigga come through here trying to blaze something, we're going to war. Nigga I keep heat on me," said Tye confidently. He turned on the trimmers while Tone continued to speak.

"Yeah ah-ight. That mafuckin deuce deuce you be carrying ain't gone kill nothing but bad breath because once a nigga see you pull that little shit out, he ain't even trying to talk anymore. He just gon rush you," he said laughing.

Tye turned Tone around and around in the barber chair giving him an eyeful in the large mirror.

"What you want Tone, you fake ass Al. B. Sure," he asked.

"My usual 1 ½ with the grain. I gotta keep my shit spinning son," said Tone patting his head.

Tye proceeded to cut Tone's hair and ended up making him look like a million dollars.

The phone in Tonia's room rings…

"Hello," said Tonia.

"Damn Ma, you're not playing. You're picking up the phone on the first ring and all that," said Tone.

"Whatever."

"Come downstairs now, I'm outside."

"Do you want me to call a taxicab Pa?" asked Tonia, oblivious to the Big Boy Lex sitting outside.

"Nah, a car is out here waiting already."

"I'll be down in a minute Pa." She hung up the phone and double checked herself in the mirror in her living room, popped a piece of bubblegum into her mouth and headed for the elevator. Tonia stood in front of the building looking for Tone. Tone beeped the horn of the brand new Land Cruiser. Tonia realized the beeping was for her and she headed for the back of the SUV. Tone rolled down the tinted window and yelled, "Get in the front Ma!"

"Whose truck is this honey? Is it a rental?" she asked as she entered the vehicle.

"Nah, this is us Ma. This is what I wanted you to see. I just bought her today," said Tone beaming.

"For real?" asked Tonia excitedly. "Do you owe anything on it Pa?" she added as Tone pulled off.

"Yeah, but not for long," replied Tone. "I'm gonna pay it off, but I want the house first," he added.

"Wait, what house Pa? Are we moving in together?" she asked staring at her boyfriend.

"Be easy Ma! I'll explain everything to you on our way to City Island."

City Island is a strip of gourmet seafood restaurants about 15 minutes from the Bronx going towards Long Island. By the time they arrived at their location, Tone had told Tonia everything that had happened in the last 24 hours. He shot her curve balls here and there because no matter how close, street rules always apply. Never tell a woman all of your street business because they're usually the first ones to be questioned and the one more likely to fold and give up information.

After dinner, they headed for the hotel and spent some time in the hotel's bar area until they were ready to get into each other's pants. They retreated upstairs after a few drinks feeling hornier than a homo in jail. As soon as they entered the room, Tonia ran to relieve herself. Tone sat on the bed and slowly untied his 3 ¼ burgundy alligator shoes by Mauri. When Tonia came out of the restroom, Tone followed her lead and relieved himself as well. Tone came out of the bathroom and found Tonia completely naked. He slipped out of his unzipped pants and threw his shirt on the side of the bed. Tonia was lying on her stomach with a big smile on her face following Tone's every move with her bedroom eyes. Tone walked up behind her and lifted her at the waist putting her in the doggy style position. He then buried his face in Tonia's rear end like a scared ostrich and gently licked her like a thirsty dog in a puddle of water. After about 15 minutes, Tone repositioned Tonia so that now he was on his back and Tonia was sitting above his face giving him more access to her love button. All the while, Tonia was moaning all sorts of stuff in Spanish, while Tone continued eating like he was still at the restaurant. After Tonia couldn't take it anymore, she eased herself down and rubbed his swollen manhood around the surface of her soaked love tunnel until she reached a third orgasm. She then slid Tone's large man meat inside of her to the hilt and began to ride him like a little kid does his bicycle on Christmas day. Tonia did something with her hips that Tone can never figure out. She seemed to be able to rotate her waist without actually spinning around. Tone had half a bottle of Crystal and two coronas up in him that had his testicles numb. He made love to her for the next two hours. When Tonia realized Tone was about to explode, she jumped off him slamming her warm mouth on his shaft in full deep throat mode until the explosion was too much for Tonia's mouth to handle. However, she managed to prevent any from spilling. She continued bobbing her head up and down his shaft until he was fully erect again. Once erect, Tone put Tonia back into the doggy style position, her favorite, and gave it to her like a jackhammer until her multiple orgasms were too much. They both collapsed after the last big explosion and Tonia told Tone how she forgot to take the pill two days in a row and how she missed taking it that day on purpose. They talked some more about their promising future together and every time Tone felt a tingle, they were at it again like rabbits. They finally went to sleep at about 4 a.m. Both dreaming about reaching the stars.

CHAPTER EIGHTEEN

A round 10 a.m. the following morning, Tone dropped Tonia off at her house and told her to look for a nice place in New Jersey, close to New York City. He then paged Dev and Slick and told them to meet him in the Blue Park. Slick and Dev were already at the park so Tone let them know that he'd be there in two minutes because he was just dropping Tonia off at her building. Tone pulled up about five minutes later in his triple pearl Lexus Land Cruiser on 18" factory customized chrome rims. Tone hopped out. "What's up?" said Tone slapping his friends five with their usual greetings.

"You Tone!" said Slick. "Dev basically schooled me to what's going down. I feel good, but I'm just mad I can't ever find any moves like you be doing," added Slick.

"Fuck that. You guys are my family. I know if any one of y'all, like y'all have done in the past, would've come across a power move, we all would've been in on it. So don't sweat that shit son! One hand washes the other, and both hands wash the face. Ya heard!" said Tone. "As soon as we get with some of these people, like the first $30,000 or so that we make, we are going to all snatch up houses somewhere on the outskirts of the city. Like Jersey or something, so when we start making a lot of money, these fucking crab ass niggas around here won't be all up in our business. I already have wifey checking up right now, so we should all be bouncing real soon. Hopefully, all in the same neighborhood too," added Tone.

"Slick, you're going to have to really step up your game and let Faye know the rent doesn't get paid when her man is sitting up in the house all day pillow talking," said Dev, looking at his friend.

"I know Dev. She be tripping for real. She thinks since she's pregnant, she can keep me on lock. She's definitely going to have to fall back for now if she wants to shine with the kid later. Matter of fact, she and I are going to have a long talk tonight. Seriously! I got this under control, ya heard! Let us three worry about getting this money, and I'll worry about my broad," said Slick.

"Alright then, I got the stuff in my mother's house right now so let's holla at some of these people," said Tone as he pulled out his cell along with the list and started dialing numbers.

Meanwhile…

The phone rang …

"Yes, who's this?" asked Beissy.

"Me girl, Tonia."

"Oh, what's up Tee. I'm sorry, I didn't recognize your voice," said Beissy as she sniffled.

"Are you okay Bess? You sound like you're crying," asked a concerned Tonia.

"I am, but I'll be okay," she said wiping tears from her eyes with her hands.

Tonia insisted, "No. Talk to me girl."

"My mother is tripping as usual. She said that she was going to kick me and my three children out again. I'm getting tired of it. Everyday I come home from work, it's the same shit. 'Bitch do this! Bitch do that! Bitch get out! Bitch you need to take care of these damn kids!' Then their father never comes around with his sorry ass. Plus, they're bad as hell. This shit is driving me crazy Tonia. So imagine having a crackhead for a mother who's stealing your money and your children's food stamps. I can't take it anymore. I swear I can't."

"Bess, I feel so bad," said Tonia hoping to calm her friend's nerves.

Beissy shook her head. "Don't."

"I wish I could help you but right now I can't. But this is what I'll do, as soon as I find something, my room will be open over here at my mother's house. And you know she loves you to death, and your kids. Anyway, you can stay here, three kids and all. That way you can relax a bit until you can get yourself together. Okay?"

"Tonia, you're so sweet," said Beissy cracking a smile.

"You're my girl. How much are they giving you in food stamps now?" asked Tonia.

"A hundred and eighty dollars. They're talking about $60 every two weeks for each child. Those children eat $60 up in one meal," said Beissy laughing over her tears.

"Listen Bess, you and the kids get dressed. I'll be over in a minute. I want y'all to help me find my new place."

"What, you moving girl? When?" asked Beissy excitedly.

"Whenever I find something."

"Who? You and Tony?"

"Yup!"

"That's so sweet. He is so responsible, loving and caring. You're a really lucky girl. You really are. I'll be dressed in a minute okay? Me and the kids. Just come on through whenever."

"Okay."

"Bye bye."

Beissy and Tonia had been friends since childhood. Beissy met and fell in love with her children's father in junior high school and her first child was born when she was just 14. Two more children soon followed. Beissy's boyfriend, Robert, six years her senior, turned out to be a no-good alcohol-drinking lazy bum. He never gives her anything for their three children, and when he sees them in the streets, he just yells at Beissy and complains about their attire. Beissy's had enough. Anymore might break her.

Back at the park with Tone and his friends...

Half of the names on the list had messages left on their voice mails. The other half briefly got acquainted with their new connect. As soon as Tone finished up a conversation with the last person on the list, one of the numbers he left a message on now appeared on his pager. "Somebody just paged me back! It's the fourth number on the list," said Tone. "Dude might be from the Middle East or something because his name is Daoud Muhammed," added Tone.

"Fuck it, call him back and see what he's talking," said Dev. Tone dialed the number from his cloned cell phone. Tone and his crew kept cloned cell phones in case anyone was listening. The cloning reduced the risk of getting traced to an exact location.

"Asalamulaikum!" answered a man with a Saudi accent.

"Walaikumasalaam," responded Tone. The Middle Eastern man remained silent for a moment thinking to himself, "What the fuck!" Tone's friends knew Tone became a Muslim during his three-year stint up north but they never knew he knew how to speak and understand Arabic. He let them know as he covered the phone that he just responded to a greeting that the Muslim guy gave him.

"You American?" asked the man on the phone.

"Mi amigo es tu amigo," said Tone indicating that he was now associated with the Spanish contact.

"Oh, okay. Do you have now?"

"Yeah."

"Let's meet for food. Come to my restaurant on 118th. I'm in South Jamaica Queens. We talk more when you get here."

"Alright Ohk, I'm on my way now. I should be there in like half an hour. Who do I ask for when I get there Ohk?"

"Just ask for Big Daoud. My American friend Big True will be looking out for you. Okay. Oh, the store is called Jebril's," he added.

"Alright Dah. Asalamulaikum Ohk. Shukran," said Tone thanking the Muslim guy in Arabic.

"Walaikumasalaam Ohkie. Afwan!" said Big Daoud before hanging up.

Tone, Dev and Slick responded to a few more calls that evening, and by the end of the night, four meetings turned into $200,000. Daoud purchased a kilo of the heroine for $110,000 and three other customers, two of them white guys, David Shetlig, Pete Danby and a West Indian guy named Dylan, each purchased a kilo a piece of cocaine at $30,000. Tone and his crew realized they were going to need a money machine if the currency was going to be coming in abundance like it did tonight so they contemplated driving up to the "Spy Counter" shop in Mt. Vernon. They decided it was too late so they made plans to go through there the following day. They counted up the money three times just to make sure it was all there. Tone kept the money with him that night while Dev and Slick retreated into the night. Tone now at home realized that he never called Tonia back who also paged him while he was meeting with Daoud. The night was still young so he gave wifey a call.

"Hello Ma?" said Tone.

"Damn nigga, you forgot about me already?" asked Tonia.

"Nah Ma, you already knew the deal. I was handling business when you paged me. But what's up anyway?"

"I found us a hot little spot in Teaneck, New Jersey. It's like 15 minutes from the roller rink, and like 15 to 20 minutes from the George Washington Bridge. It's close to the city like you suggested. It's a condo Pa, in a gated complex-like community. On its grounds is a Sizzler restaurant, a pool, a gym, a party room, and a tennis court. I took a cab out there earlier. Beissy came with me. I liked it so much, I put down a deposit on it with my credit card. I know you'll like it, so don't get mad that I snatched it up without you. The condo has a full basement, two bedrooms, 2 ½ baths, a patio with a cage out there I guess for a pet or something. We also get a two-car garage. What else? It's nice though Pa, I can't wait until you see it. Oh yeah, you told me we can afford something nice and they wanted $850 a month. I gave up two months' rent, plus security so you have to give me $2,550 to put back into my account before the check bounces. They didn't even need a large down payment."

"That's cool. I'm home chilling right now Ma, so get something to wear for tomorrow and come over and stay with me tonight. Plus I want to talk about if you can somehow help Slick and Dev get cribs in the same complex."

"Beissy's having problems with her mom and Robert. Her mom is still using crack and stealing all of Beissy's money and belongings, and Robert is just as lame. When we move, I'm going to let Beissy keep my room at my mother's until she can get herself together."

"That's real supportive of you Tee. I guess when you get here, we can go straight to the bank's drive-thru so that the money will be processed early in the morning. So come on Ma and I'll see you when you get here."

"Alright Pa, I'll see you in a minute." She hung up and got ready for another night of fucking and sucking. On the low, Tonia's a freak, but Tone is the only one who has the privilege of seeing that side of her.

The following day, Tone, Tonia, Slick, Fay, Dev and Frenchie all hopped up in the Land Cruiser and headed out to New Jersey to get a close up of their new homes. Slick and Dev wound up purchasing condos for themselves inside the same complex, but in different sections for privacy reasons. Afterwards, they headed out to purchase cars for Slick and Dev. Slick ended up getting a four-door teal green Tahoe because he'll need the room for his family, and Dev purchased a '94 BMW M-5, triple black with deep dish 18" factory racers on it. They then split up to different furniture stores to find the best living room and bedroom suites available. The three of them stay in competition, but it's friendly competition. It keeps their relationships healthy and fresh. The women are also excited about their new homes. They decide to stay in the empty apartments and sleep on the plush carpet while their men tend to their own business. The furniture is scheduled to arrive first thing in the morning and everyone is all hyped up about their new lives. God is good, thinks Tone. As if nothing can go wrong.

CHAPTER NINETEEN

Third quarter, 1995...

"Dev, are you trying to go shopping?" asked Tone as they play Play Station in Tone's basement.

Pressing the buttons aggressively on the joystick, Dev answered, "Yeah, where are we trying to go?"

"I don't know. It really doesn't matter to me. As long as it's not here in Jersey," said Tone moving his joystick around as if it would help him operate the game better.

"Why?" asked Slick.

"Because, all they have is preppy pretty boy shit," said Tone.

"Let's go to the 'S & Ds' on Nostrand Avenue in Brooklyn then," said Dev.

"Or what about Century 21 on Houston Street in downtown Manhattan?" asked Slick.

"Like I said, it doesn't matter to me, but if niggaz need a hint to make up their minds, 'KPs' on 145th Street got all the new Air's and fitted's. And they got stuff for females like Baby Phat and all that. You know when I get, Tonia gets as well," said Tone.

"We're riding with you Tone, so wherever you're going, we're going too," said Slick.

"Let's go then," said Tone.

They all hopped up in Tone's Land Cruiser and headed to Manhattan's Washington Heights section. They parked on the corner of 145th and Broadway and went up into "KP Sportswear."

"Hey my friend!" said a Spanish guy assumed to be the manager or owner sitting atop a ladder.

"What's up Poppi!" said Tone.

"What can I do for my very good friends?" asked the man giving the trio a dose of his sales pitch.

"We're going to look around for a bit and if we need your help, we'll holla," said Tone as Slick and Dev scope out the latest summer and fall wear.

"Okay my friend, holla."

"Ayo shorty," said Slick to a cute Spanish store clerk. "Let me get two pairs of white on white, low top Air Force One's, size 10 ½. Let me get all of these jean shorts right here in a 40"," said Slick pointing to a row of eight different styles of jean shorts. "Match me up some t-shirts with all of the shorts and give me like four packs of socks too. Give me two navy blue size 7 fitted World Series Yankee's hats and that'll be all," he added.

"Excuse me shorty," said Dev. "You may as well get me the same things. My foot is a 9 ½ though and I'm a 36" waist. Make my t-shirts 3 XL, not 7 XL like his," said Dev laughing along with the store clerk. "And I don't want any hats."

The store clerk was writing everything down because she knew she couldn't blow the sale or she'd blow her bonus.

"Holla at my man, he's buying too. For two!" said Dev

looking at Tone with a smile.

"May I help you sir?" asked the store clerk walking over to where Tone stood.

"Yeah, uh, let me get two pairs of the white on white Air's, size 8, but make one of mine high top. Give me the high tops with the removable straps. Not that new shit. I like my straps to hang like an O.G. And Give me two more pairs, same one's but a 5 in girls." Tone looked at the store clerk and realized that she was about the same height, weight and shape as Tonia. "Aye, do you have any of those jeans that you have on that fits you just like that?" Said Tone pointing to the store clerk's legs.

"Over here." She pointed to about 11 different brands of women's jeans that were form fitting.

"Well give me one pair of all of them. The same waist and length that you have on now. Pick me out some nice tops to go with them too. My wife's chest is a little larger than yours is, but she'd probably buy a size smaller to show off her damn cleavage so give me the same size shirts that you'd wear. My head is a little larger than Big Boy over there so I'll need a 7 ½ in the Yankee hats. I want two baby blue ones, a navy blue one, a yellow one, and two red ones. Give me matching Doo Rags to sport underneath the hats too. Oh yeah, I hope y'all know that you two forgot boots," said Tone loud enough so Slick and Dev could hear him.

"Get 'em for us," yelled Dev while he flirted with another female store clerk.

"Give me four pairs of those beige two-toned sole Timbalands right there," said Tone pointing to your traditional construction boot model. "Matter of fact, I need four pairs in an 8, four in a 10 ½, four in a 9 ½ and give me two female pairs too. Make those a 5 for wifey. Give me two pairs of Pepe jeans shorts. Thirty-eights. Give me two Mecca's too. The same waist. And give me two pairs of light grey 3XL sweat pants with the pockets. Give me two pairs in a medium too. Same color. Oh yeah, and two of the navy blue sweat pants, same order. That's it Ma," said Tone. The female returned with the amount printed on a small piece of paper. It read $2,975.00.

"Yo Poppi," yelled Tone to the manager.

"Aye," he answered.

"No tax right?"

"No tax for you Papa," Said the manager smiling.

Tone gave the girl $3,200.00, a $225.00 tip. She bagged up everyone's stuff and offered to carry their bags to the truck for them. When she and Tone got outside, she said, "My name is Lorna. I'm here everyday until 9:30 p.m. The number to the store is on the bag. My number is on your receipt. And it does-n't matter if you have a wifey. I love being the mistress. Call me anytime Poppi Chulo."

Tone accepted the number and the trio hopped in the SUV and drove off. Dev bragged about his upcoming episode with the Spanish girl he just met in the store. Tone tucked the receipt in his pocket with no intention of using it to call the girl to make her his mistress. Antonia is his wifey and her other side, Tonia, acts as his mistress. She's everything balled up in one.

Later at Tone's house...

Life is great, thought Tone and his crew. The drugs were getting low, and it was time to meet with the connect again.

"Dev, after you count up $500,000, put the rest to the side so one of us can add it to our stack. As a matter of fact, for time sake, Dev, you work the money machine, run each stack through three times to make sure what you've counted is cor-rect. Slick, either you or I, it really doesn't matter to me, but one of us can take the stacks from Dev, write down the amounts on this piece of paper," said Tone as he held up a single piece of paper and a pencil, "then we'll pass it to the free person. That person will then rubber band the stack flat to insure space. Then they'll place the stack into one of these three bags," said Tone as he pointed to three large camcorder bags on the floor, "until all of them have the 1.5 that we need to re-up with. So who'll do what because Dev, if you don't want to use the money machine, any one of us will switch with you. I just figured since you're more of an electronics man, in case the machine jams up or something, you can perhaps fiddle with it to get it popping again," continued Tone.

"It's all good, I got the money machine," said Dev.

"Fuck it, I'll rubber band the money up and add it while you stack 'em in the bags with your neat freak ass," said Slick to Tone.

"Alright, empty all the money from all the trash bags right here in the middle of the floor. It's mostly $100's and $50's and probably like 100 to 150 thousand in $20's. We would have been looking like the beginning of the second Scarface tape when Tony and them were bringing several garbage bags of cash into that one bank if it were in all 20's, 10's, 5's and singles," said Tone.

"Word!" said Slick.

After three vigorous hours of counting and recounting the money, the crew bagged up $500,000 neatly into each bag and ended up with an extra $210,000 to split for themselves. They figured one quarter of the total amount of the drugs going to them wasn't bad.

"Whatever them Poppi dudes are getting this shit for, if they're not growing it themselves, they're probably getting it for dirt cheap so I know they're alright," said Slick.

"Fuck it, we're happy," said Dev.

"Alright, let's holla at these people and get things on a roll. We still got paper to chase fellas," said Tone before whipping out his cell phone and speed dialing the connect.

CHAPTER TWENTY

T he phone rings …

Ring! … Ring! … Ring! …

"Si!" said a Spanish voice on the phone.

"Qué pasa hermano, es tu amigo, Antonio!" said Tone.

"Si, yo se. ¿Everything okay hermano?"

"Si! We're trying to, you know, holla again."

"Okay. I'll send somebody to pick you up in two hours. Where should they meet you?" asked the connect. Tone thought for a minute. Never was he going to let them dudes know where he lived although the possibility existed that they probably knew where all three of them lived anyway, but to be on the safe side, he analyzed for a second what would be the smartest way to travel with a million and change in tow.

"Hey, you have your peoples meet me at 170th Street and Riverside Drive in like two hours."

"Si hermano! Uno, seite, cero, Y Riverside Drive. Dos

hours. Yo tengo esto! A jello tassicab con la numero eleben sisty on it will meet you there in dos hours," said the Spanish guy in his best English. Tone figured getting across the George Washington Bridge shouldn't be that hard. It's just flying around New York that may be the problem. One hundred seventieth and Riverside Drive isn't that far from the bridge and it isn't too deep into Manhattan either.

"So what are you going to do Tone? Do you want us to come with you?" asked Dev.

"That's a lot of money right there," said Slick.

"I know, but I'm good. I'll drive the Caprice to sort of blend in with the police. Plus I'm bringing Saharah and her 13 children with me," said Tone.

"Who the fuck is Saharah?" asked Slick.

Patting his waist, Tone said, "My desert nigga!"

"Oh that's right."

Two hours later Tone pulled up to 172nd Street and Riverside Drive and found a parking spot. He exited the vehicle leaving the bags of money and his gun inside the car with the vehicle unoccupied. It was less than likely that anyone would suspect it of anything. As Tone approached 170th Street, he noticed the yellow cab with the number 1160 printed on the side of it. He inconspicuously walked by the cab peering into its window with the corner of his eye and he noticed a Spanish guy reading a newspaper behind the wheel oblivious to everything else happening around him. Tone continued by and proceeded to 169th Street, scanning and looking for anything suspicious. Tone got to 169th Street and crossed at the corner to avoid drawing attention to himself from the cab driver or anyone else watching. He then walked back to 172nd Street and Riverside and approached the Caprice. Out of nowhere, a white Crown Victoria and a beige Chevrolet Caprice came flying down 172nd Street blaring its mini-siren with two white plain clothes officers in each vehicle gripping the dashboard as they made the sharp turn onto Riverside Drive. Tone immediately stopped in his tracks and his eyes followed the police cars as they screeched down Riverside Drive apparently on a call or something. The police cars raced south past 170th Street and continued heading downtown at full speed. Tone relaxed and quickly popped the trunk to retrieve the bags with the money in them along with picking up Saharah and discreetly tucking her into his waistband. He calmly strolled toward the livery cab and hopped into the back seat. The cab eased on into traffic and headed toward the highway ramp at 181st Street. Tone relaxed and felt he was in good hands now that he was in the company of the connected.

CHAPTER TWENTY-ONE

After negotiating the same deal with the connect, Tone simply went about the same procedures returning home as he did making it to the connect. Once home, he and his crew got back to business as usual. Slick met up with one of the white customers, Dave, who purchased another kilo of cocaine. They made the exchange and as soon as Slick returned to Tone's house, he got a page '911' from Dave.

"Ayo Tone, that white dude Dave keep beeping me off the hook, '911'. Do you think he wants another brick already? Or do you think it didn't weigh right?" asked Slick.

Shrugging his shoulders, Tone spoke up. "I don't know Slick, call him back." Slick dialed the number and got a busy signal, obviously from Dave continuing to page. Slick redialed and this time the phone rang.

"Hello," said Dave answering his phone on the first ring.

"What's up," said Slick.

"Hey, what is this shit? What the fuck is this man? I treat

you guys with respect. I bring you into my home and let you have dinner with my family and this is what I get! You guys are outta your fucking minds bringing me some shit like this! You black guys must be crazy or something! I called my friend!"

"Yo, yo, yo, yo, hold on! Slow the fuck down white boy! You're a fucking white boy, not a thug. Fuck you, you mafucka! I'll come through that ol' little house on the prairie shit and lift you and that picket fence in the air with some hollow tips," said Slick, upset now. "All my stuff be legit! Don't ever accuse me of doing anything foul. I always brought your ass straight up shit. Mafucka!" added Slick.

"Well I want my money back then or something, and I apologize for getting all upset with you guys, but shit man, I thought I had my usual shit and bam!, my fucking nose is bleeding all over the damn place, like my face was on its period or something. I can't let my wife and kids see this shit! It pissed me off man!" Before Slick could go on, Tone told Slick to tell Dave that we'd holla at him in a minute. The connect had paged '911'. Tone called him back wondering if the connect already knew what had happened.

"Hello," said Tone.

"Meet me at the cathedral on 175th Street and the Grand Concourse in the Bronx. Come to confession booth #3. I'll be there in 10 minutes," said the Spanish guy. Click! The line went dead.

"Tone, what did he say?" asked Dev.

"He's trying to meet right now for some reason, I don't know. More than likely, it's because of the bad work. Somebody else probably complained and he realized he hit us with some fucked up shit."

"So what up, how are we supposed to meet up?" asked Dev.

"Dude is trying to meet right now at some church or something on the Grand Concourse. On 175th Street somewhere."

"Is there a church up there? I'm not sure," said Slick asking himself the question and then answering it for himself.

"It might be, I don't think Poppi would give us false information," said Tone. "Come on Dev, take us over there," he added as they walked out to Dev's BMW.

"Ayo Dev, where is that 'Clue Summertime Shootout CD'? What number is it in your changer?" asked Slick from the back seat of the car.

"That's the newest joint I purchased so I put it in the #1 slot." Dev fiddled with his state of the art Pioneer system and turned the volume up so that the bass thumped ... "Tommy Gun Dunn and Money Mike pulled a heist, him and light knocked off the same jewelry store twice/Ice dripping, his women sipping, Rum and Lemon/ watching Niggaz body language and funny rythms/ I detect who pants too big, those ain't your size yet/hang with them kids, you ain't ready for wise guys yet ..."

"Ayo, that nigga Nas is killing that track son," said Slick excitedly as he bounced around in the rear section of the sport sedan.

"Hold up," said Tone flipping the CD to another song. "Hold on, here it go. The illest!" ... "Who shot ya! Separate the weak from the obsolete, hard to creep them Brooklyn streets/it's on Nigga, stop all that bickering beef/I can feel sweat trickering down ya cheek/ya heartbeat sound like Sasquash feet, thundering, shaking the concrete..." "You hear my nigga Biggie! Brooklyn Nigga! We brought the east back! What!" said Tone excitedly as they continued down the Grand Concourse.

"Shut up nigga! You ain't even from Brooklyn. Biggie and them ain't no real gangstas anyway. He's rhyming about his man's experiences. Here's a real thug!" said Dev flipping the CD to another song ... "Out on bail fresh outta jail California dreaming/soon as I step on the scene I'm hearing hoochie's screaming/fiending for money and alcohol, the life of a West

Side player where cowards die/we all ball ..." "Yeah Nigga! Pac! What Niggaz!" said Dev as he blasts the 2Pac song dissing the east coast. Dev turned the radio down and the three of them get into an argument about who's the hottest dude in the rap game. As Tone peered out the window, he noticed a guy who looked familiar. "Dev! Dev! Hold up! Make a U-turn!" Said Tone tapping Dev's arm.

"Yo what the fuck! What happened?" asked Dev as he makes the U-turn.

"Yo, you see dude right there with the dreads and the squeegee in his hands?" said Tone pointing.

"Yeah," said Dev zeroing in on the guy.

"Pull over, let me holla at him for a minute. I know son. We were locked up together somewhere. Matter of fact, we were upstate in Coxsackie together in '92. I think he was from Buffalo or Albany or something. One of them country towns upstate. But he went hard up north. He was a sneak thief up there. Snatching up everything that wasn't nailed down. That's how I met him. He was about to get punished by the Muslims up there. I saved his ass and me and him started kicking it. We ended up getting cool but he got in some more trouble jerking off to the C.O. or some wild shit and got moved." They pull up. "Ayo money!" shouted Tone. "Where do I know you from?" Tone was leaning out the passenger side window.

"You don't know me from nowhere money," said the dreaded guy. Holding the squeegee by his side.

"Were you up north before?" Tone was trying to reassure the guy that he meant no harm.

"Why?" said the guy nervously.

"Matter of fact, Nature! Yeah, Nature! What's up, it's me, Tone! Remember, Pretty, T-O-N-E," said Tone trying to refreshen the guy's memory.

"Oh yeah, Bx. Yeah, little Bx. What up my nigga?" said Nature sounding more confident and comfortable now.

"Shit! What's up with you? Yo, where was you from upstate?"

"Rochester dog."

"Oh yeah, the Rock. What are you doing down here in the city? You're a long way from home, aren't you?"

Nature walked over to the car and leaned into the passenger side window. "I'm fucked up. I'm on the run right now. I'm trying to hold court in the streets this time too Tone."

Tone thought for a quick second.

"Dev, give me some dough," said Tone. Dev passed Tone about $2,000. Tone gave Nature the money with a handshake to follow up. "Hold your head Nature. Stay up," said Tone.

"No doubt Bx. Good looking. That was well appreciated dog. I gotta love you for that one. Be easy y'all, and be safe," said Nature banging his fist against his heart symbolizing the appreciation for the love Tone showed by dishing out the money.

Tone sighed and leaned back into his seat. "Damn. Shit be rough for people sometimes," said Tone as they drove off. Slick and Dev remained silent feeling Nature's pain.

They arrived at the cathedral several minutes later. They entered and both Slick and Dev took seats on either side of the cathedral and pretended they were worshipping. Tone headed straight for the confession booths. He entered #3.

"My friend," whispered the Spanish guy. "We don't need any problems Señor. Sometimes things happen. Most of the time we can fix them, sometimes we can't. Fortunately, Davey Boy understands, so we're able to fix this one. Under your seat are two more kilos of cocaine. Bring them to him now for no charge at all. However, this time I want back 1.52 altogether. Next time, you talk to me first before you react. Comprende?" said the Spanish guy firmly.

"Yeah ah-ight," said Tone, as he walked out of the

booth. He headed out and Slick and Dev followed behind him noticing the brown bag in his hands.

Taking a quick look behind him as he walked, Slick began the questioning. "What happened Tone? And what's that?" asked Slick.

Opening the passenger side door, Tone replied, "I guess Elvis must be an important customer because not only is he getting reimbursed double, for free, we're the one's paying for it. Dude told me to bring him back $20,000 more than last time," said Tone holding the door for Slick to climb in the back seat.

"So that's one million, 520 thousand right?" asked Dev taking his seat behind the wheel. He and Tone closed their doors at the same time while Dev put the car in first gear. Tone placed the drugs in the stash box.

"Yeah. Fuck it though. We live and we learn y'all," said Tone.

Tone realized that clientele is very important when you're in any kind of business, and treating your customers right was a priority. You have to do good business in order to stay in business.

After dropping the coke off to Dave, the trio headed back home to relax.

"Ayo Tone, are you trying to stop off and buy those sneakers your brother wanted before he goes upstate?" asked Dev.

"Fuck him. My mom just sent him like $300 Sunday. He's either getting high or gambling because he be calling for money like that every month and my mom be hitting him off because she doesn't know how it is in jail. I mean true, we definitely be needing money and all, but $300 is a lot every month. Especially for a person in jail. It's not like he's even up north yet. He's still on Riker's Island and their spending limit is like $70 a week. That's about $280 a month, but still, he's not spending $70 every commissary," said Tone.

"He might be trying to save some of that dough because you know when you first get up north, you need commissary immediately," said Dev changing lanes to avoid congestion.

Lowering the volume on the radio, Tone continued, "I know. But I really think he just be using my mom. He doesn't even call her on a regular basis. Plus his ass wrote me the other day trying to curse me out like I'm some lame nigga or something. I have the letter with me as a matter of fact. Listen to this shit…

Tone pulled out the letter, unfolded it and read it to his friends.

"Dear Tone,

How's my little brother doing? Fine I hope. How's Mommy and the family? Tony, you be on some bullshit with me for no reason. You're getting all that money now and you act like I'm not your big brother. You need to get your mind right and stop acting up. Write back soon. And send a money order with it.

Big Eugene."

Tone closed the letter, placed it back in the envelope and placed the envelope in his back pocket.

"That's my brother so he's going to always be alright. Just be appreciative, you know," said Tone adjusting in his seat. "I was planning on sending him a big package once he touches his upstate facility anyway. I was going t buy him some Timbs, some Nike Air's, sweatsuits, food packages, books, magazines and send him like $2,500. That way he can lay off my mom for a long while."

"I'm feeling that right there Tone," said Dev.

The trio drove quietly for a while then Slick spoke up. "Drop me off at my crib. I'm gonna fuck with Faye for a minute. What are you two going to do?" he asked.

"I'm going to go and fuck with my bike. My throttle has been locking up on me lately. Fuck around and kill myself trying to wheely," said Dev exiting the ramp on the George Washington Bridge.

"I'm just gonna go to my spot and chill. Probably wait for some more customers to page us," said Tone.

They hit their condo complex and dropped Slick off first because he lived the closest to the entrance than any of them. Dev dropped Tone off at his apartment and pulled around to his own court. When Tone finally entered his crib, his home phone was ringing. He rushed upstairs to answer it and saw Tonia on the bed crying like a baby. "Ma, what's wrong?" He yelled.

"Tony, why. Why Tone?" said Tonia over her tears.

"Why what? Hold on, let me answer this phone real quick."

CHAPTER TWENTY-TWO

S lick knew that Faye would usually be out shopping. He figured he could prepare a romantic dinner for the two of them, something he'd been wanting to do since he first met her. Since he has laid down the law to her, he kept a topic of discussion. Slick opened his apartment door and realized that Faye must have left the radio playing before she went out. He turned the radio off and realized that someone was home. He heard a peculiar sound so he proceeded upstairs to investigate. As he approached the top of the steps, he could hear what appeared to be someone repeatedly making a hissing noise.

"Sssss! Sssss! Sssss! Sssss! Sssss!" went the voice.

Each hissing sound was about two seconds apart. As Slick got closer to his bedroom door, which was slightly open, the hissing sound became much louder and clearer. What Slick saw through the crack of the door made his stomach feel like he just swallowed a ton of bricks. He peered through to get a closer look in case his eyes deceived him. He saw his pregnant girlfriend Faye, lying on her stomach with her legs hanging halfway off the edge of the bed with the tall dark-skinned guy that bumped into him at the 'Jimmy Jazz Sportswear' store, Jayson, giving Faye what appeared to be about 11 ½" of man meat up her ass. Something Slick had never done or thought that Faye could even handle. With every long, deep, slow stroke, Faye released the hissing sound. Slick stood there for a moment trying to digest what he was seeing and when he snapped out of his trance, he quickly darted back downstairs to the living room. He reached into the center console of his living room sectional and retrieved the 40 caliber semi-automatic pistol he kept there for protection. He darted back upstairs and this time saw Jayson pumping hysterically into Faye's rectum while Faye buried her head into the pillow. At the moment of climax for Jayson, Slick kicked in the bedroom door, eyes watery, voice crackling and shouted, "What the fuck is going on Bitch! Are you fucking crazy?"

Faye deliriously popped her head up from beneath the pillow with her eyes so wide it looked as though she had no eyelids. Jayson couldn't quite get a grip on himself yet because the orgasm he held back for the last hour was too overwhelming. But when they both realized that Slick had 3 ½ pounds of nickel-plated death in his hands, they immediately snapped out of porno mode and into reality.

"Slick. I, I, I'm sorry! I don't…," said Faye stuttering nervously as she crawled from underneath Jayson with her butt hole stretched to the size of a golf ball slot.

"Shut the fuck up Bitch!" screamed Slick. "I should blow your fucking head off you fucking whore! You slut Bitch! Shut the fuck up! Don't say shit! Don't say one word! You say something else, I'll make your head look like your asshole bitch!" added Slick obviously steaming now. "And you," said Slick aiming the gun at Jayson, "you fucking, you fucking motherfucker! You want to come into my house, you faggot! You want to come into my house and be with my wifey? Is that what you fucking want you fucking dead man? Huh?" said Slick as Jayson tried to interrupt with an "I didn't know." Slick then pulled the hammer back to add a little emphasis to his thoughts and told the man, "Shut the fuck up. And sit your ass right there!" motioning with the weapon for him to sit beside Faye. Faye began pissing on herself because she didn't know if she'd live or die and Jayson had sperm all over his legs from when he pulled out of Faye's gaping rear end. Slick reached for the phone and speed dialed Tone.

Tone entered his house and noticed his girlfriend crying. Before tending to her, he chose to answer his phone.

"Hello," said Tone.

With his gun in one hand aimed at his hostages and his telephone in the other, Slick screamed into the phone, "Get over here now Tone! This dude is crazy!" said Slick more angrier now.

"What's up Slick? What's going on?" said Tone looking at his hysterical fiancé.

"There's a guy in my house, get over here now. You and Dev!" said Slick as he hung up the phone and stared at Faye. The only woman he truly ever loved and would give the world to if he could now brought tears to his eyes from her deceit. Tone and Dev arrived at Slick's house together and when Slick heard them fumbling downstairs, he yelled down to them, "Up here yo!"

"Can I please just cover myself up at least?" asked Faye now crying like a baby.

"Oh now you want to cover your nasty ass up. You was-n't thinking about that when homeboy over here was knee deep into your ass," said Slick looking at Jayson as Dev and Tone made it to the top of the steps. "Hold up y'all. Put that sheet over your whore ass. Now bitch!" screamed Slick.

She quickly pulled the sweaty sheet over herself. "Look at this shit!" said Slick to Dev and Tone as they both positioned themselves to see inside the bedroom.

"Ayo what the! Hell no!" said Dev.

"Slick!" said Tone brushing past Dev.

Slick looked his friend up and down, then returned his gaze to Jayson and Faye and said, "What."

Concerned that something crazy might happen, Tone reached his hand out to Slick and asked, "Are you alright?"

"Yeah I'm ah-ight! But these two mafuckas won't be in a minute," said the overweight member of the group.

"I feel you dog on that but right here isn't the place. Dev, take that from Slick and keep them sitting right there like two statues. Either one of them move, leave 'em stinking!" said Tone looking at Dev.

"Slick, come here for a minute. Come here," said Tone a little more firmly now. Dev kept the drop on the porn stars while Tone and Slick retreated to an adjacent room.

Wrapping his arms around Slick, Tone spoke calmly to his emotional compadre. "Listen to me Slick. I know how you feel. There is no explanation for this. But Slick, not here. We can tie up both of them maggots and bring them to the woods if you want to. Feel me! It's up to you dog," said Tone pausing in front of his friend. "It really might not be dude's fault because he probably didn't know. Maybe he did, I don't know. But whatever we're going to do, we can't do it here." Slick walked back toward the bedroom with Tone watching him very closely. Slick brushed past Dev who was taunting Jayson.

Faye raised her head and noticed Slick approaching her so she began screaming at the top of her lungs. "Noooo! Noooo! Please! Please, noooo!"

"Shut the fuck up you stupid bitch! Shut the fuck up!" said Slick as he grabbed some of the sheet that Faye had covered herself with and tried to shove it down her mouth to keep her quiet.

"Bitch, you're lucky that you're pregnant." Those

must've been the most relieving words Faye had ever heard in her life. She now felt a sense of relief because she knew her life had been spared. "But for how long?" she thought.

"You, Homeboy, come here. Now!" demanded Slick. Jayson walked nervously to an adjacent room with Slick.

"Sit down," said Slick. "What's your name?" he added.

Jayson bowed his head and spoke in a low tone. "Jay Boog."

Slick slapped him and said, "Your real fucking name."

"Jayson Jones," he said nervously.

"Tone," said Slick keeping his gaze on Jayson.

"What!" said Tone approaching the duo.

"Dig in dude's pocket and see if he has any type of identification on him," said Slick motioning Tone to search the man's garments. Tone found a wallet inside Jayson's pants and tossed it to Slick.

Slick read the information on the guy's driver's license aloud. "Jayson Jones, 1183 Webster Avenue, Apartment #2B. Do you live there alone?" asked Slick.

"No, my wife and daughter live with me," said Jayson unable to look Slick in his eyes.

"You're married?"

"Yeah."

"So what the fuck are you balling my wife for?" asked Slick.

Scared, Jayson sighed and spilled his guts. "I used to fuck with her before. She used to be a dancer and I was like her favorite customer. One day I offered her $500 to spend the night with me. She accepted and liked the way I freaked her. After that, she said that I can have some whenever I wanted to, anywhere, at any time, for no charge at all. Then about six months ago, we lost contact. I seen her the other day on Fordham Road, she took my number and here we are. But I swear to God on my daughter that ..."

"Shut up! Put your shit on and get the fuck out of my house. If I catch you around here again, your wife will become a widow," said Slick cutting him off in mid sentence.

Jayson ran back into the room, put on his pants and his shoes, grabbed his shirt and ran out of the house.

"I'll handle Ms. Fuckems later! Y'all can go home now. I got it from here," said Slick walking his friends to the door.

"Are you sure?" asked Tone.

"Yeah, I'm sure." Slick stared at Tone. His eyes told his friend that he'd be okay.

They left and 15 minutes later while at Dev's house, Tone called Slick to make sure he was okay.

The phone rang and Slick immediately answered it.

"Hello," said Slick.

"Are you okay?" asked Tone.

"Yeah, we're alright. That bitch is in the shower right now. We talked about some things and after she gets out of the shower, I'm going to drop her ass off at her mom's house. I'll take the Tahoe and lug all of her shit tonight."

"So what's the status with y'all?"

"We're finished. It's over. I'm going to let her have the baby, then I'll take my kid and move on." Dev and Tone sucked their teeth quietly and told Slick to be easy. "Yo, I'm going to holla at y'all after I drop her off and get my head right."

"You sure you're alright Slick?" asked Dev on the other telephone in his house.

"Yeah, I'm good," said Slick more confidently now.

"Yeah, that's the nigga I grew up on franks and beans with," said Tone trying to cheer up his upset friend. "You know dude is innocent, just make sure things are tight on your end," added Tone.

"I got that. She knows better now. She knows how I get down."

Tone wanted so bad to say "If she knew how you got

down, why the fuck she got another nigga's dick up in her," but he felt anything may trigger his homey.

"Alright then, we'll holla," said Tone. And they hung up with each other. Slick began loading the truck with all of Faye's belongings. Faye eventually walked out of her former residence closing the door behind her, hopefully for the last time as a resident there. She placed a pair of $400 Gucci shades that Slick purchased for her over her eyes to hide the bags she got from crying so hard. They hopped into the Tahoe and began their journey back to the Rotten Apple. Slick put on "Just Me and My Bitch," a song by the Notorious B.I.G. to rub in Faye's face how a true bitch is supposed to carry it. Slick thought to himself, "How the fuck did this bitch play me without me knowing it?" The CD played on as they headed back to Manhattan. It's a half hour ride, but to them, it seemed like a lifetime.

CHAPTER TWENTY-THREE

Tone remembered Tonia was crying when he left so he raced back to his place from Dev's.

He entered his house and called out his girlfriend's name. "Tonia. Tonia," said Tone running up the stairs.

"I'm in here Pa," said Tonia sniffling from inside the bathroom.

Opening the door he asked, "Is everything okay?"

"No. Everything is not okay." And the tears began to flow again as Tonia pointed to a newspaper sprawled across the bathroom floor. "Why honey? Why would she do that?" asked Tonia crying harder once again. Tone picked up the paper. A New York Daily News. Front page read: "WOMAN AND THREE CHILDREN DIE IN TRAGIC HOUSE FIRE!" STORY ON PAGE THREE! Tone looked at Tonia and saw her sitting on the toilet seat cover with her head bowed in her hands crying softly now. He opened the paper to page three and saw the story.

"FOUR ALARM BLAZE RIPS THROUGH BRONX HOUSING APARTMENT!" He read on: "At approximately 3:27 a.m. this morning, the first 911 call was made from a female caller stating that she smelled smoke coming from a nearby apartment. She was then told to knock on the person's door and when she touched the knocker, she almost burned herself. She screamed for help and ran back to the phone and explained what had happened. The operator was tracing the call as she waited and dispatched a signal to a nearby fire department. The caller, hysterical now, ran through the building banging on neighbor's doors screaming for help. Many tenants responded, and some called 911, but the door was too hot to open. People outside the building said the blaze looked like something out of a movie. One witness, according to a source close to the family, said if anyone was in that apartment, the remains were probably gone with the smoke. When the firefighters finally got the blaze under control, they entered the premises and found a woman and three small children in the bathtub with the water allegedly running. Unfortunately, the water couldn't stop the smoke from reaching the family and the four of them were taken to Jacobi Hospital where they were pronounced dead an hour later. Cause of death, smoke inhalation. The woman was identified by her mom as 22-year-old Beissy Castillo. The children's names, because of their ages, were being withheld."

Tone closed the newspaper after looking at the horrific photos and took Tonia by the hand leading her into their bedroom. There the two laid beside one another with Tonia fully embraced by the warmth of Tone's arms. He caressed her and kept repeating to her that everything would be okay. After a few minutes, he assumed it was alright to speak. "Ma," he cordially said.

"Yes Pa," she responded still shaken by the news.

"Are you alright?"

"I think so," said Tonia as the tears began rolling down her face once again.

"Listen Ma, you have to be strong. Beissy would've wanted you to be strong for her and her beautiful children."

"I know Pa, but …"

"No buts, whatever the cost, we're going to make sure Beissy and her children have the best caskets, the cleanest dirt, the most luxurious limousines and the best funeral service. Everything Ma, but you have to be strong because you're going to be the one to handle everything, okay? You know her mom can't handle anything right now. She's probably having a nervous breakdown herself. So get on the phone and take care of everything," said Tone as he walked out of the bedroom.

Sitting up, Tonia asked, "Where are you going Anthony?"

"Nowhere, I'm going to run to the car for a minute and get my cell phone. I have to make a long distance phone call. I'll be right back. I'm not going anywhere. Just call the hospital and the funeral home."

"Okay Pa. I'll get on it as soon as I blow my nose and wash up."

Tone ran to his truck and retrieved his cell phone. He called Dev and they three-way Slick to see if he was still holding up. After hanging up with them he walked back to his apartment and dialed 1-315-555-1076.

Ring!

"Hello," said Tone.

"Hey Tony, how are you?" said Juanita, from her home in Syracuse, New York.

"I'm fine sis, but I need a favor," he said biting his lip.

Juanita placed her hand on her cheek and said, "Anything wrong Tony?"

"Yeah, kinda, not with me though."

"Talk to me Tony, you're scaring me. Is everything

alright at home?" she asked sounding concerned.

Looking at his watch he asked, "Do you still have your same schedule?"

"You mean four days on and four days off?"

"Yeah."

"Yes why?"

"When will you be off again?"

"Today is my first day off. I have the next three days all to myself. Why, what's up?" she asked strolling over to look at her calendar.

"Well a friend of mine and Tonia's died in her apartment from a horrible fire last night."

"Oh my gosh. I'm sorry. How's Tonia?"

"She'll be alright in a minute. It's just that this whole situation seems a bit strange." Tone began pacing the area in front of his apartment.

"What do you mean?"

"Well apparently our friend had a rough relationship with her mom, and Tonia and I were going to get her a place to stay for a while, like really soon. Anyway, it was reported that she tried to save herself and her children. Tonia thinks that our friend Beissy may have deliberately set the fire herself to escape the misery and agony that she was dealing with in her life. I don't believe someone who wants to kill themselves will do it but then try to save themselves in the process. I mean a person doesn't put a gun to their head with blanks in it if they really want the job done. You know what I'm saying?"

Grabbing her Rolodex, Juanita said, "Well because of my rank, I can make a few phone calls and arrange for me to gain access to the crime scene. I'll get on the phone right now and see what moves I can make before they start tearing the place up."

"Whatever the cost Juanita, you know I got you."

"I know, but don't worry about that right now. Take care

of Tonia because I can imagine what she's going through. And you take care of yourself too. And be careful out there. I'll call you when I'm down there and find something. Okay?"

"Okay sis, but call me anyway, even if you don't find anything. At least I'll know."

"Love you. Take care," said Juanita.

"Love you too."

"Bye bye!" she said ending the call.

"Bye!" They hang up.

Tone closed his cell phone and retreated back to Tonia's side, comforting the love of his life and thanking Allah that his girlfriend and family were all okay.

CHAPTER TWENTY-FOUR

The phone rings...

"Yo," Answered Dev.

"Yo," said Tone.

"Yo what's up?"

"Where are you Dev?"

"Right around the corner."

"You at your crib?" Asked Tone

"Yeah."

"Have you seen Slick?"

"He's right here next to me. Do you want to speak with him?" asked Dev looking over at Slick.

"Nah, I'm alright, as long as he's ah-ight."

"Yeah, he's alright. We kicked it. My man is going to be alright." Said Dev tapping Slick on the shoulder.

"Yo, do you feel like driving?" Asked Tone

"Where to?"

"The projects."

"Whatever. What's up though?"

"Beissy died last night, this morning rather."

"Where, in the projects?" Dev was surprised. He turned to Slick and made a face as to say "something happened."

"Yeah, she died in a fire. Her and her kids. They suffocated. I just want to go through there and see how everything looks up close. You know what I mean?"

"Yeah, I got you. Are we bringing heat?"   Dev shook his head and quietly mumbled "mm, mm, mm."

"Of course. We can never go back to them projects without a burner," said Tone referring to a gun. "Them dudes are too grimy in there. Remember, we were once a part of that crowd." Said Tone fiddling with his gun.

"Yeah, you're right. We'll be over in a minute to get you."

"Ah-ight."

"Peace," and they hung up.

When Tone heard the music outside his door, he looked at his girlfriend and told her he would be right back. He hopped in the car with Dev and Slick and they headed for the Edenwald Projects.

Thirty minutes later. Approximately 9:30 p.m.

The trio pulled up to the front of Tone's old building, their former stomping grounds. After seeing the horrible crime scene of their friend Beissy, Tone decided to cruise the neighborhood to see how things were going. They pulled over and sat out front of his old building. "Ayo, who's that lady in the window? I thought Mexicans lived in that apartment. That's a black older looking lady in the window though," said Slick looking up at a third floor apartment.

"Some Mexicans did live up there. I guess they must've moved out a while ago because that bitch ass nigga Black told me that his mom moved up in there. A few years ago. So I guess that's his mom or his aunt or something," said Tone looking toward the window.

"Damn, she looks kinda good from here," said Dev staring.

Glancing back up there, Tone said, "Yeah, she's all in your face too pretty boy."

"She's all in your face nigga," said Dev returning his gaze to his friend.

"Oh, she left now," said Slick also returning his attention back to his friends.

"That's because your black ass scared her," said Tone to Slick as they all began to laugh.

"Damn, it's dead out here now. There's no one walking around or anything," said Slick.

"There goes a crackhead," said Dev pointing toward a skinny dingy looking guy walking by.

"That's Basehead Dave right there," said Tone standing up on the bench to get a closer look.

"Ayo Dave. Yo Dave," shouted Tone.

The man stopped and looked in their direction. "Who the hell is that calling me? I hope you got something to give my ass, calling me like that," said Dave, trying to see who was calling him from a distance.

"It's me, Tone," shouted Tone in the direction where Dave was standing.

Focusing, Dave replied, "Oh, youngin, where you been at? Aye, hold on a minute, I'll be right back. This bitch just ran in Peaches' house with my hit," said Dave walking off.

"Aye, what's up Black?" said Dave as he walked past Black at the top of the hill. Black just ignored him and kept on walking toward the trio.

"Ayo, who is this walking over here?" asked Dev.

"That looks like Black," said Slick immediately identifying their old associate.

"That is that faggot," said Tone as they all patted their waists to remind themselves that they had pistols on them.

"Yo, what up y'all," said Black as he neared the three-some.

Pop! Pop! Pop! Pop! Pop! Shots rang out. Everyone ran.

Moments later, "Aaaahhh! Aaaahhh!" screamed a lady from a window. She ran and dialed 911.

Ring!

"Hello operator!" screamed the lady.

"Yes, may I help you?" replied the operator.

Hysterically, she began her explanation. "Yes. There's been a shooting. There's a guy lying on the ground outside my window and he might be shot. He could be dying. Please send some help fast."

The operator began tracing the call. "Where are you calling from ma'am?"

"I'm at 1187 East 226th Street Drive."

"And what is your name ma'am?"

"My name is Latonya Little."

"And you say a man got shot? How do you know he was shot?"

Nervous and upset, Ms. Little screamed, "Because I heard the shots goddamit! Just send some fucking help already," said Ms. Little as she hung up the phone.

As a small group of people gathered around, Ms. Little ran downstairs and tried to aid the victim.

"Move back everyone. I'm a nurse," yelled Ms. Little.

"Oh my gosh! You can't even see his face," said a bystander.

"Hell no, his face is covered with mad blood. He must've got hit up in the head piece," said another bystander, a guy this time.

"Is he still breathing?" asked another lady.

"Yeah, his stomach is still moving. You see it right?" said the guy pointing.

"Sir, can you hear me? Can you hear me sir?" asked Ms. Little not wanting to move the victim. "Sir, who did this to you? Who did this?" she continued. She was leaning over the victim looking for visible bullet wounds.

The ambulance along with a couple of police cars pulled up and began moving everyone away from the victim. Crime scene officers arrived and put yellow tape up everywhere. The paramedics placed the body onto a stretcher and loaded the victim into a waiting ambulance. They headed for a nearby hospital as the police canvassed the area for clues and witnesses.

On the George Washington Bridge, a black BMW M-5 raced toward New Jersey. Its destination, Teaneck.

"Ayo, what the fuck just happened?" asked Slick. His heart was still racing.

"That nigga just came out of nowhere. I didn't even really see him until he got up on us," said Dev. Focusing on the road.

"Fuck him. He shouldn't have been fronting," said Tone. "As long as we're ah-ight, okay. Just thank Allah for that," added Tone as the threesome rode the few minutes left that it took to get home in silence.

CHAPTER TWENTY-FIVE

The next day, the news reported the shooting!
DAILY NEWS! PAGE 9
MAN SHOT DEAD IN BRONX HOUSING PROJECT!
"**L**ast night at approximately 9:35 p.m., a 23-year-old man, who was subsequently identified this morning allegedly by his mother as Antron Little, also known as Black in his neighborhood, was shot five times in the face. The police have no suspects, no witnesses and no motive for the shooting as of yet. Police are still searching for clues.

In other news …"

Everyone including Tone, Dev and Slick has read the newspaper, and by now have asked themselves a million questions. The trio was concerned about whether or not Basehead Dave would report anything.

Four days go by and Tonia got a phone call at her New Jersey home.

Ring… Ring…..Ring
"Hello" Answered Tonia

"Hello. May I speak with Antonia Nunez. Asked an unfamiliar voice on the phone.

This is she," replied Tonia. Tonia turned the chicken she was frying over so that the other side could cook.

"This is Federal Agent Roberto Delano of the FBI's Special Homicide Unit. I need to ask you a few questions Ms. Nunez. My partner and I will be over shortly to discuss this matter in a more formal manner."

"Is there a problem officer?" asked Tonia not knowing what the call was about and hoping that Tone was okay.

"Well, that's what we would like to find out Ms. Nunez. We're on our way," said the agent hoping he had found a break in the case. Tonia immediately called up Tone who was in the middle of a transaction and explained to him what had just transpired. He told her to remain calm and when the agents arrive to stay quiet. Not to say a word about anything without the presence of an attorney. He then gave her the number of a lawyer and told her when they get there, if they have anything to ask, for them to refer it to her attorney.

The agents knocked at the door moments later.

"One second please," called out Tonia as she headed toward the door. She opened the door and found two well-dressed agents at her doorstep.

"Hello, are you Ms. Antonia Nunez?" asked Agent Delano already knowing who she was from viewing a photo of her driver's license using their special identity match program.

"Yes, I'm Ms. Nunez," said Tonia, remaining calm. "May I help you with something officer?" she added. She held her door open wide enough so the officers could get a whiff of the marvelous dish she was preparing.

"Well, we'd like to ask you a few questions ma'am, if you don't mind," said a black agent who stood 6'2", 240 pounds, with a short Afro and no facial hairs.

"Well if you guys would like to ask me anything, I think

I should call my attorney first," said Tonia to the agents who now looked at one another.

"Well ma'am, it's just a few questions, but if you insist on calling your lawyer, you have him call us," said Agent Delano, an Italian cop who resembled the white detective on the hit T.V. series "Miami Vice." He then handed her his card, thanked her, and left.

As the agents got into their vehicle, the black agent, Agent Michael Williams, looked over at his partner, shrugged his shoulders and said, "Seems pretty cool to me."

"Yeah, too cool, don't you think."

"If she knows anything, do you think she'll talk?" Asked Agent Williams.

"If she knows something, she'll have to talk," said Agent Delano as they drove off.

Tone's mom paged him 911. Tone called her back from behind the wheel of their 1990 Honda Accord hooptie.

Ring ... ring ... ring!

"Hello," Answered Mrs. Wheeler.

"Hello Mom, what's up?" asked Tone as Mrs. Wheeler answered her phone.

"The police have been by here today Tony asking for you," said his mom sounding upset.

"The police? For what?"

"How the hell should I know? I thought you weren't in those damn projects anymore!" she shouted.

"I'm not Mom. Maybe it's for something that happened a while ago. Did they say anything?"

"No honey, they just left their card and said if I heard from you to tell you to give them a call. Do you want the number?"

"Yes Mom, give it to me." His mom read both the fax number and the telephone number to him and added, "Your brother also called again as soon as the police left."

"What did he want now?"

"Probably nothing. We talked for about 20 minutes and that was it. The police even acted sarcastic by asking me how Eugene was doing. I guess they were the ones who locked him up or something too."

"Maybe. And what was Eugene talking about Mom? Was he asking for money again?"

"No, he didn't ask for any money. He just asked where you were staying now. He said he needed your address as soon as possible."

"You didn't give it to him, did you?"

"Of course not Tony! I'm not stupid!"

"What else Mom?"

"He also said he may be able to put in a motion of some kind to get his case dismissed."

"I thought he was sentenced already."

"I thought he was too. I don't know about that court stuff Tony."

"Alright Mom. Thank you. And stop worrying."

"Boy, as long as you're not in my sight, I'll always worry."

"Okay Mom. Bye."

"Bye sweetie, and be careful."

They hung up and Tone thought to himself, "What the fuck is Eugene up to?"

CHAPTER TWENTY-SIX

The next day at Tone's house. The phone rings...

R ing ... ring ... ring!

"Hello," answered Tonia.

"Hello Antonia?" said Juanita unsure of to whom she was speaking to.

"Yes, may I ask who's speaking?" Said Tonia cordially.

"It's Juanita."

'Oh hi, how are you Nita?" said Tonia calling Juanita Nita for short.

"I'm fine, and you?"

Sighing she said, "I'm alright now, but I recently went through something losing a friend."

"Yeah, I heard. Are you sure you're okay?"

"Yes, I'm fine. Anthony's here. Would you like to speak with him?"

"Yes, thank you."

"Hold on," she said covering the mouthpiece of the phone.

"Alright sweetie."

"Tony! Tony!" yelled Tonia. Tone was in the living room watching television.

"Yo!"

"The phone!"

"I got it. I got it, hang up," said Tone picking up the other phone in his house.

"Okay, bye Juanita." Continued Tonia.

"Bye Tonia, and you take care of yourself, and my brother."

"Okay."

"Alright y'all," said Tone anxious to speak with his sister.

"Shut up," said Tonia before hanging up.

"Yeah, hello," said Tone.

"Yeah." Replied Juanita

"Did you find out anything?"

"Yup, it was hard because I guess they're trying to appoint a new fire chief down here. I did manage to find out a few things. Tony, I think your friend was on something and apparently did commit suicide."

"Why do you say that?" Tone walked over to the living room window and peeked through his mini blinds.

"Well strangely enough, what appeared to be a crack pipe and a lighter were found near where the fire apparently started. Someone, I'm guessing your friend, deliberately started this fire by igniting the fire on a living room curtain and dropping the crack pipe as she tried to flee. The location of the crack pipe and the lighter helped me determine that it fell accidentally and the way the remains of the curtain lay on the floor, I was able to determine that it was started by the lighter also found at the scene."

"Did you have any help obtaining that information?"

"No Tony. You don't have to keep on paying money to everyone. I did it alone."

"Listen sis, if you can, do not report this to anyone. I don't want people to know this woman was getting high off drugs. Then all the sympathy is gone. You know what I mean?"

"Yeah, I got you. Do you need me for anything else Tony?"

"No, that's it Juanita. Thank you very much. I really appreciate it."

"I'm sorry that you had to hear that Tony."

"Yeah, me too. I'm glad that I heard it though. You just made my day."

"Alright, and don't worry about me, I'll be on my way home in a minute. I'm already a day late. I called in and explained that I had a family emergency. I'll be alright. And remember, I'm here when you need me."

"Of course."

"Bye Tony."

"Bye Nita."

Tonia looked at Tone as he placed the phone receiver back on its base. "Tony, is everything okay?" She asked noticing a serious look on his face.

"Yeah, I'm ah-ight Ma. Hey! Where'd you say Beissy's mom was staying at right now?" said Tone walking toward her.

Touching his cheek, Tonia answered, "She's at a hotel that the Salvation Army provided for her. The Paradise on Boston Road and Gunhill. Why?"

Tone reached for his keys and said, "No, I just wanted to know if she was okay."

"Oh, alright. Are you leaving again Pa? You know Beissy's funeral is in two hours."

"Oh yea, that's right. I'll be back in time. If not, have Dev or Slick drop you off and I'll meet you there."

Back in New York...

Tone sat in his Chevy Caprice behind the dark tint and watched as Ms. Castillo ran in and out of her room apparently running back and forth purchasing crack with the money that the local Salvation Army was raising for her in neighborhood grocery stores and video shops, etc. Tone put on a pair of surgical gloves, a skullcap and approached her room. He knocked at her door.

Boom ...... Boom ...... Boom!

"Yes," she answered.

"Room service," said Tone disguising his voice. He cleared his throat.

"Wow, I didn't order room service," said Ms. Castillo walking towards the door surprised.

"I know ma'am. I did," said Tone keeping his head low.

"You did, who are you?" asked Ms. Castillo opening her room door.

"It's me Scotty, here to beam your ass up!" said Tone pushing the door as she opened it.

"Oh my gosh! Please! No! I don't have anything!" said Ms. Castillo nervously backing up to her bed as Tone closed the door behind him. Tone sat on a chair, pulled out a 9 mm and screwed a silencer on the tip of it.

"What is this, young man? Please! What's going on?" said Ms. Castillo, terrified and sitting on her bed with a crack pipe beside her.

"Just tell me why?" said Tone aiming his gun at her.

"What? Why? Why what?" she stuttered.

"Why the kids?" he asked.

"What are you talking about?" said Ms. Castillo not even remembering that she just lost her grandkids.

"Bitch, you know exactly what I'm talking about. Why the fuck did you kill those kids in that fire?" At that point, all the fear left inside of her tiny body let her know that her life was about to come to an end. She positioned her face in a non-expressive manner and sat at the edge of the bed.

"Just get it over with, would you," she pleaded.

Tone aimed and gave her one to the forehead. As she fell back, with her brains on the wall behind her, Tone stood over her and said, "That was for Beissy, this is for her children," he said as he put three more slugs into her torso. He then turned and left the hotel unnoticed.

Tone pulled up to the funeral home on 226th Street and Bronxwood Avenue, just a couple of blocks from the Edenwald Houses. People packed the small funeral home to pay their last respects to Beissy and her three children. Tonia picked out four beautifully carved white caskets with gold trimming. One adult sized casket carrying Beissy's body lay to the far left of the other three caskets carrying her children. All the caskets lay in sized order. Family and friends from all over filled each pew with loving memories of the children they all lost. After a long speech given by Reverend Jimmy Calhoun, Antoinette, Tone's sister, sang a capella of "Boys To Mens' hit "It's So Hard To Say Goodbye." Everyone sat in total silence as she sang, and afterward, the floor was open for anyone who wanted to share their touching words about Beissy Castillo and her three children. Antonia made her way to the podium and when she turned to look at the four caskets behind her, her legs got weak and she dropped to her knees screaming out "Whhyy! Whhyy did you take her from me?" Tony ran over to Tonia and carried her wilted body out of the funeral home and rushed her home to her mother's house.

"Ms. Nunez, please watch her. She couldn't take seeing Beissy like that. Stay with her as I go to the burial to make sure that she is buried correctly," said Tone walking his distraught girlfriend to the sofa in her mother's living room.

"Okay Antonio. I take care of my daughter," said

Tonia's mother in her best English. Tone dashed back outside to find Dev and Slick waiting in Slick's Tahoe.

"Tone," said Dev.

"What," said Tone entering the vehicle.

"Is she okay?"

"She will be." Tone pulled the rear passenger door closed. Slick put the truck in Drive, stepped on the break pedal, turned around to tone and said "So what are you trying to do because everyone is beginning to pull out so that they can head to the cemetery."

"I'll ride with y'all. I need to clear my head anyway." Tone made himself comfortable in the back seat.

"So what? Are we going to the cemetery?" asked Slick.

"Yeah. You might as well go from here. We'll just meet everyone up there."

Tone, Dev and Slick rode out to the Woodlawn Cemetery off of Jerome Avenue in the Bronx. The four Castillos were buried right beside one another, and each of them was given a tombstone. Beissy's read:

Beissy Castillo

1974-1995

"An Angel from God!"

Her children's tombstone read something similar. Everyone rolled out quickly and quietly and Tone and his friends were right behind them.

"Tone, where to?" asked Dev.

Tone reclined in his seat and said, "Let's go back to Jersey and just chill for a bit."

The trio headed back to their Jersey homes and for the next three days, they took in everything that had happened.

CHAPTER TWENTY-SEVEN

Three days later…

Tone, Slick and Dev hit the old neighborhood again to see if they could find Basehead Dave for some more Black Talon bullets. They pulled up to 228th Street and Laconia Avenue in the Honda Accord. The pizza shop right across from the Edenwald Houses where everyone hung out was half empty today.

"Isn't that Dro right there near the phone booth?" asked Dev pointing.

"Yeah, that's that big forehead mafucka. He probably got some $5 slabs of crack stashed up in the coin slot. Dro is grimy like that," said Slick. They exited the car and stood around.

Dro spotted the trio and began walking in their direction. "Oh shit, let me find out you guys are finally coming back to the hood," said Dro, a short dark-skinned dude with a low haircut and a big forehead. "I wonder what brings the three stooges back to y'all's stomping grounds," he added.

"Have you seen Basehead Dave around here?" asked Tone.

"Nope. I think Dave stopped smoking or either he's locked up or something because he don't be around anymore. Why, what's up, he sold y'all a broke pistol or something?" said Dro with a laugh.

"Nah, I'm just looking for him." Tone stared at him. Excited, Dro Said "Yo, where are y'all niggaz at anyway? V.A. or something? Y'all three are probably in N.C. somewhere getting that Carolina's money."

"What makes you think that?" asked Tone.

"Man, them motherfucking Crown Vic's and Caprices have been flying around here left and right, and y'all names have been coming up."

Slick interrupted, "How do you know that?"

"Because a few niggaz got picked up already for questioning and are talking about how the Po Po keep asking about y'all. Like you guys done killed the president or sold him some drugs or something. Plus, everyone is talking about those Black Talon bullets y'all be carrying."

Surprised, Tone said, "Word! Dev, Slick, let's bounce. Yo Dro, I'll holla at you later, good looking." The trio hopped back in the Honda. "Dev, get us up outta here!" said Tone as Dev made a U-turn.

As the Honda made the turn, the guys found themselves facing a road block of about 30 police cars and 60 policemen waiting to begin target practice. They put the car in park.

Retrieving his bullhorn, an agent began talking into it. "Don't fucking move! Put your hands where I can see them Anthony! Your friends too!" said Agent Williams. Tone killed the engine. "Put y'all hands out of the window so these racists mafuckas won't have a reason to kill us! Dev, is the Ruger put away?" asked Tone.

Forcing his hands out of the window Dev spoke to his

friend. "No doubt Tone. We don't have to worry about them finding that in here. Remember, the guy who installed our stashspots put that anti-thing on them so the authorities won't be able to locate them."

"Alright then, if any of us gets out of the interrogation, go somewhere on the low until everything blows over, alright?" said Tone looking at his two friends.

"Ah-ight," said Slick and Dev at the same time.

"Step out of the fucking car with your hands still where I can see them!" said Agent Williams, now in a much closer position. Tone and his friends slowly exited the vehicle with their hands never leaving the air. Oblivious to what the cops were saying, the three friends lowered themselves to the ground lying on their stomachs with their hands still raised above their heads. Dev had an itch in his trousers and without thinking, he attempted to scratch himself. The last thing Dev heard was, "He's going for something!" Shots rang out. Pop! Pop! Pop! Pop! Pop!

"Stop shooting! Stop fucking shooting! Now!" yelled Agent Delano, the one in charge. Tone looked over at Slick and saw Slick looking back at him with tears in his eyes. Slick then looked over at Dev. Tone followed his eyes and couldn't believe what he saw next. Dev was lying beside him shaking with one eye socket clearly ripped apart. Dev was trying to say something to Tone but the only thing that kept coming out of his mouth was globs of blood. Dev began to choke and Tone didn't even care anymore. He crawled over to Dev and grabbed his head and yelled, "What the fuck! Why the fuck did y'all have to shoot him! He didn't have anything! Get him some help! Get him some fucking help you pigs!" Dev stopped shaking. His stomach also stopped pumping air. Dev was dead. "Noooo!" screamed Tone. About 12 officers walked over to Tone and his dead best friend and dragged him off of Dev. They didn't even handcuff him. They let him walk himself to the patrol car where he began swinging at the police cars, breaking two of their windows. Six officers had no choice but to subdue the emotional young man. Meanwhile, six other officers handcuffed Slick and placed him in a separate patrol car and drove off with him. Agent Delano couldn't do anything. The damage had already been done.

"It was me who yelled he's going for a gun sir," said a young white uniformed officer. "I, I…" with a wave of hand, Agent Delano cut him off. "I don't want to hear it. I want a report on my desk immediately!" he added as he and his partner boarded their own vehicle. "Clean this mess up! The media is going to have a field day with this one," he said to his partner.

"I guess he had it coming," said Agent Williams, the up front Uncle Tom. Agent Delano looked over at Williams and said, "We were supposed to arrest these guys, not shoot them. We're officers of the law, not madmen on the street," said Delano giving his partner the hint to chill out. They went to One Police Plaza, Federal Police Headquarters, in lower Manhattan, and Williams told the help to "Get these scumbags outta here!"

They went upstairs to the interrogation rooms.

"Sit down Anthony," said Agent Delano. Tone sat in a chair adjacent to the officer and listened to him rambling about nonsense. "I'm sorry about your friend. He didn't deserve to die. No one does. Not even Black," said the agent looking for Tone to react. "You guys don't own the streets Anthony. We do! We're the strongest gang out there! Can't you see that?" said the officer leaning in Tone's face. "We run the streets! You guys get your little drug money, buy yourselves a few guns, pop a couple of your own brothers and sisters, and then you think you're untouchable. Well I got news for you Tony, you've been touched!" said Agent Delano.

"Yeah, we got your ass!" said Williams.

"Back off Williams!" shouted Delano. Anthony knows

when good cop, bad cop routine comes into effect, this time, however, he can tell that Agent Williams has his own agenda.

"Listen Anthony, it's over! Your best friend is dead, and your other friend is facing life right along with you. An individual lost his life from some Black Talon bullets that you guys carry. One of you guys did it," said Agent Delano. Right there Tone knew the agents didn't have anything concrete.

"Think about your son Anthony. Your mom. Would you rather them prepare a death certificate for you if you went all the way with this or simply prepare a visiting form for one of our penitentiaries we have? It's up to you Anthony. It's your call," said Agent Delano as he backed away from the interrogation table. Agent Williams placed his hand on his chin while sitting in one corner of the room. Agent Delano was behind Tone and out of his sight. Tone sat there with his eyes locked on the floor not saying a word. He was thinking about Dev and all the good times they had together. A thought came across his mind and he chuckled to himself. The agents noticed it as well as the officials recording everything from an adjacent room and everyone tensed up. Tone was thinking about Dev's favorite movie, "The Usual Suspects." It's about a man that walked right out of the authorities' hands, but was wanted for multiple homicides. Tone's face tightened up and he looked over at Agent Williams, he then turned around to see Agent Delano behind him imitating Agent Williams' movements.

Tone spoke softly, "Delano!"

"Yes there Tony." Agent Delano looked up from where he stood. "Are you ready?" said Tone keeping his head down.

"Ready for what Tony?" said Agent Delano still behind Tone and looking at his partner with a smile.

"You guys wanted me, now y'all have me. Y'all got me, and my best friend! One dead and one alive. But I'm not giving you guys shit unless y'all let Slick go."

"Hold, hold, hold, young man. We're the one's who call

the shots here," said Agent Delano, now picking for something. Tone remained silent.

"Anthony. Anthony! So now you're going to give us the silent treatment," said Agent Delano as he waited for a reaction from Tone. The agents conversated quietly behind Tone because they realized that their shot at an admission would be missed.

"What is it that you want Tony?" asked Delano circling Tone.

Tone liked the way they called him Tony. It made him feel like he was Scarface.

"Okay, okay. If you can guarantee us that you'll cooperate, we'll let your friend go. But if you fuck us, you fuck yourself Anthony," said Delano stopping and standing behind the suspect.

"Let him go," said Tone before he lowered his head again letting the agents know that he meant business. The agents knew that they didn't have anything concrete to hold both of them so they thought they were the ones getting over. An admission, for hardly no work at all is a blessing, so they scrambled to arrange the release of Slick who had no idea of what was going on. All he knew was that one of his friends were dead, and to keep his mouth shut. Moments later, a uniformed officer retrieved Slick from a holding cell and escorted him to the front desk. A desk sergeant told Slick he needed his signature.

"I'm not signing shit," said Slick with his arms folded.

"Well if you don't want your property back, don't sign anything! Apparently your friend was weak and he cut a deal to let you go. He gave us what we wanted."

Slick was confused, but he knew Tone, and he knew that Tone always had something sly up his own sleeve. He just wished Dev could be there with them. He signed the necessary paperwork and retrieved the items confiscated from him earlier.

"Can I have my friend's items?" asked Slick holding his hand out.

"You can't have your friend's belongings who was killed because we need that for evidence, and you can't have your friend's things that are still in our custody because we'll need that for evidence in his case. So have I answered your question?" asked the desk officer sarcastically.

Slick just looked at the man and walked away. As soon as Tone saw his friend pull off from an office window, he knew that once his man hit that highway, he was home free. He then returned back to his seat.

"Well young man, give us what you got for us," said Delano.

Looking at Delano, Tone said, "Get your little tape recorders and notepads and shit out. I got something for y'all to write down that y'all can print in tomorrow's newspapers. But before y'all do that, I'm hungry. All this drama got me starving," he said with a smirk.

"Hungry?" said Delano. "Well what do you want?"

"I want a Wendy's Chicken Fillet with cheese, no tomatoes. A Biggie fry and a large pink lemonade."

"Don't just stand there, get the man what he wants!" ordered Delano looking through the see through mirror where all the recording was taking place. Fifteen minutes later, Tone's food arrived. Eight minutes after that, his food was gone. He cleaned himself up and said, "I'm ready."

The agents tapped the window and grabbed chairs and notepads and settled around the table.

"Well Anthony, go ahead," said Delano anxiously. Tone cleared his throat and looked straight into the camera and shouted, "Fuck y'all! I want to see my lawyer!"

Agent Delano realized what just happened, jumped out of his seat and kicked Tone in his face, forcing him to the floor.

He began to shout, "Get somebody on Slick! Find his ass now!" Everyone was scrambling and the room was a big mess. Everyone knew they'd been had.

CHAPTER TWENTY-EIGHT

Slick thought to himself, "What terminal did we park in?" Slick drove straight from the precinct to LaGuardia Airport. After realizing the seriousness of their lifestyles, the three of them set up an escape route in case they ever needed to leave town in a hurry. They purchased three Town and Country minivans and equipped them with stashspots that were stocked with identification, cash, prepaid plastic and a 9 mm Ruger. They knew in case they were being tailed by air, the aircraft wouldn't be able to get close to the airport, and the inconspicuous minivans parked in long-term parking wouldn't attract attention.

Slick remembered, "It's three of us, we parked in terminal three, row C." Then he remembered, "Dev is dead, it's two of us now," Slick said to himself. "I can't go back to Jersey, and I ain't going to Faye's house, but I have to stay close to my man no matter what the plan was." Slick warmed up the van and pulled out of the parking lot mumbling to himself, "I love you Dev! I love you too Tone, hold your head brah!"

At the Federal Court Building...

"Anthony Wheeler! Anthony Wheeler!" shouted a court officer at the Manhattan Federal court holding pens.

"Right here," shouted Tone waving his hand through the bars.

"Your lawyer's here." The court officer, a frail old white man with black hair, escorted Tone to an area where attorneys and their clients can discuss their cases.

"Mr. Buckman, how are you?" asked Tone as he was locked into the booth with his attorney.

"I'm fine Anthony. How about you? How are you holding up?" Said Mr. Buckman giving Anthony a firm handshake.

"I'm alright. Who called you and told you I was here?"

"Well apparently your girlfriend, Tonia, called my office and my secretary, Ms. Homes, immediately paged me. I made a few phone calls and managed to catch you before arraignment." Tone thought about how on point Tonia always was. No matter what the situation called for, Tonia was always one step ahead of everyone, even Tone sometimes. Another reason why he loved his girlfriend unconditionally.

"Good! That's cool! How's it looking so far?" asked Tone.

"Well we're in the premature stages right now so it's still too early to tell, but it seems like they may have a witness of some sort. At arraignment, I'll put in a verbal motion for discovery and we'll see what we're working with from there. Look Anthony, this is a serious case. First of all, the retainer you left with me is more than enough so I'll put my investigator, Mr. Spiegel, right to work. But because of the nature of this crime, I don't think the judge will grant bond. We'll ask for a bond hearing which will basically give us extra time to do whatever and it will at least be on record that we requested it, but don't look forward to it. The judge, the Honorable Judge John Fargus, who has been appointed to preside over this case, is a fair man. He'll take into consideration any and everything from both sides. You'll more than likely be housed at the Metropolitan Correctional Center until trial as well. I predict your family and friends will be in the courtroom waiting for you to be called. After the proceedings, I'll go and explain to them what is happening. Now remember, don't say a word to anybody. I'll do all the talking here in court. And when you get to MCC, I repeat, do not under any circumstances, discuss your case with anybody. Now do you have any questions Anthony?"

"Why is this a Federal case and not state, Mr. Buckman?"

"Well apparently, the victim was killed by a particular slug released from a special bullet that is not available on the market anymore. Black Talons are bullets known to kill people instantly. A statement made by a maker of those bullets once said, 'Even if you got shot in the torso on the operating table, your chances of living would be less than 1%.' Anything black market is serious Tony. Do you understand now?"

"Yes sir. But aren't you going to ask me whether or not I did it? Doesn't that matter to you Mr. Buckman?"

"Anthony, what matters to me is getting you the best defense that I can possibly give you. That's my job, and that's my interest."

The court officer motioned to the two of them that they were next. They entered the court room and Tone immediately spotted his mother, his girlfriend, Dev's mom, Frenchie, Slick's mom, Faye, Jane who is Slick's other baby momma, all in the second row of the empty courtroom. Tenequa, Tone's son's mom, walked in from returning from the restroom and joined everyone else. Everyone started crying when they saw Tone looking disheveled. The proceedings were quick and brief. The media was barred from the courtroom, but the hungry news people waited outside the door for anything they could eat up.

Before Tone was escorted back to the holding cell, he told Mr. Buckman to tell Tonia that he'd try to call her that evening. If not, early in the morning. An hour later, Tone was removed from the holding cell and driven a few blocks down from the courthouse to the Metropolitan Correctional Center. Tone always knew the possibility of going back to prison existed, he just never thought it would be Federal prison.

CHAPTER TWENTY-NINE

Tonia paid for Dev's memorial service. Dev's mom wanted him to be cremated and she also had his ashes placed in a platinum vase in her China cabinet on a shelf next to her cremated mother in her living room.

The Metropolitan Correctional Center…

After getting processed in an area of the MCC Facility known as "Receiving and Departure," Tone was given a bedroll which included a dark grey wool blanket, two white sheets, a pillow case, a pillow, one tube of toothpaste, a toothbrush, three shaving razors, a tube of shaving cream, two bars of soap, and a bottle of roll-on deodorant. Tone was then escorted to a housing area known as 5-Block, the A-side.

"Excuse me sir! Sir!" said a black female officer who looked to be in her mid-twenties with long straight black hair and large breasts, set inside of an officer's station otherwise known as the "Bubble."

"Yes ma'am," said Tone stopping at the large glass plated office.

"May I have your I.D. please," she asked.

"Oh yeah," said Tone as he passed his identification card through a small slot at the base of the window of the Bubble.

Looking at his name on his I.D. card and referring to her papers, the officer kindly said, "31-Cell, top bunk," and passed his I.D. card back to him. Tone scoped out the place that would be his new home for a while and noticed four phones spread throughout the unit. People were scattered about, some were working out doing pull-ups on a nearby staircase, some were playing cards at several small tables, and the rest were tucked into two small T.V. rooms watching music videos and what appeared to be a movie. Tone got to his cell and found a black guy with long dreadlocks sitting at the table in the cell writing a letter. Tone had prior experience so he took it all in stride.

"Eh mon, ya iree," said the dread to Tone as Tone straightened up his bunk.

"Yeah, I'm ah-ight." Said Tone looking over his shoulder.

"Ya ungree? Me just make me food. Do ya heat dumplin dread?" said the guy in his West Indian accent.

Looking up, tone laughed and said, "Yeah, sometimes, but I'm ah-ight though. I'm good. I appreciate it though." He then continued tightening the sheets on his bed.

Tone's cellmate decided to put his paper and pens away and said, "Well listen Star, me give you some time to yarself so dat you can get a bit com-for-tahble. Ya get ungree, me leave some in me plate," said the Jamaican guy pointing to a small plastic bowl with a secured top on it. "Take it! A black mon cyan't wahlk ahround all dey with no food pon im stomach. I go now. Dem ave a microwayve pon de corner of de unit," he said pointing. "It's tree a dem. Iree Star. Safe mon!" and the dread walked out, but before he closed the door, he turned around and said, "Me name Junya, but everybody say June," then he walked out. Before Tone tightened the last blanket on his bed, Junior's friend, a black American guy with short dreads, stopped by.

"Ayo kid, what up?" said Junior's friend, 5'10", 245 pounds.

Holding out his hand to offer his friendly salutation, Tone responded with a handshake as the guy began to talk.

"Yo, my name is Dog ah-ight. Junior's my man. He's mad cool too so y'all should be ah-ight together. You need anything? Soap, shower shoes, deodorant? I got soups, whatever. I'm in 2-Cell. My room stay open." Dog was being generous because it's the way he was treated when he first came to jail as well.

"Aye Dog, what dudes be doing in here to stay busy?" asked Tone trying to familiarize himself.

Placing a book in Tone's door to keep it open, Dog began to elaborate.

"It all depends youngin. You see me, I'm 240, but I ball all day long. Ask anybody around here, 'Yo what Dog do all day?', and they'll tell you that all I do all day is ball. 'Cause that's all I do, I ball. That's me kid, all day. But you got your gamblers, dudes who play cards. You know, Spades, Pinochle, Casino, regular shit. Rummy, 500, everything. Then you have your Flex Wheeler dudes. Those are the cats that you see doing the 8,000 pull-ups over there, and can't fight a lick," said Dog as he pointed to six dudes doing an around the world workout consisting of pull-ups, pushups, and dips in the corner of the unit.

"You're bugged out Dog. Talking about dudes can't fight a lick," said Tone feeling a sense of relief from the humor.

Looking around, Dog continued, "They can't! Dudes is soft. Let me tell you, dude right there with the wife beater," said Dog pointing to one of the six dudes working out with a tank top on. "Dude let a homo punish him. I mean the gump beat the shit out of this dude. Big man thinks because he could do sets of 25 that people are scared of him. Then he wants to walk around all day long with no shirt on, and it's chumps in here. So I guess the homo must've been trying to catch and caught dude's eye, dude got all loud with the gump and homeboy just started swinging on him."

"Who? The dude swung on the chump?" asked Tone surprised.

"Nah, the gump stole on dude. Then he stomped him out and started yelling at him, 'You're my bitch nigga, I can have you if I wanted to!'" They both began laughing. "Oh yeah, you got your idiot box heads that stay up in the T.V. room all day too. I mean literally all day. As soon as they clear the 6 a.m. count and crack them doors, pewn! Dudes is up in there setting their chairs up. You got dudes who write 1,000 letters all day, and don't get no mail. And them fake Hallmark dudes who be making cards drawing and shit. You know, like a birthday card for your girl or someone. You know what I'm saying?"

"Yeah. No doubt. I just did a bid. My shit was state though. I was up north."

"Where were you up north?"

"I was in Green first. Then fucking around with them young niggaz, I tried to cut a kid in the barbershop and homeboy told on me so I went across the street to the Pen."

"My man was in Green. Rick. A kid named Rick. Light skinned dude. From Long Island. He cut hair. He worked in Industries, but he used to cut hair in the unit on the side. He might've went home early because he won his appeal. I don't know."

"He don't sound too familiar," said Tone trying to recollect.

"Anyway, they have them little rap dudes. Yo those little dudes be rapping all day in that T.V. room right there," said

Dog pointing to a T.V. room that displayed music videos on its screen. "I like them little dudes though. They be having me dying in there sometimes. It's like 10 of them. Just going at each other. It's lil Jimmy. He call himself Jimmy Da Saint. He from Philly though. But he's nice. Don't sleep on them Philly cats. Then it's this kid named Patience from Connecticut. He's nice too. He be telling stories with his shit like Biggie. Oh, my lil man Inch go hard son. Kid is from the Bronx. You might know him. Y'all favor each other a little bit too. He rhymes all day. Son definitely be repping for the Bx. He write books and all that. Them young dudes got a lot of talent but they want to run around carrying guns all day."

"Yeah, they're burnt out. Plus, it's rough on the streets right now. Guilliani got the city on lock, locking you up if you sneeze and don't cover your mouth. Then Pataki keeping you up north for damn near your whole sentence it seems like," said Tone.

Extending his arm for another handshake, Dog said, "I know. Ayo, I'm a let you finish getting your things together. If you need anything, give me a holla. You now where I stay at. If I'm not around here, I'll be in the gym, balling."

Returning the gesture, Tone said, "Ah-ight then. I appreciate that Dog. One!" said Tone telling the guy to peace out.

"One," responded Dog.

"Ayo Dog."

"Yo," said Dog turning around.

"Any Muslims in here?"

"Right there at that last table," said Dog pointing to a table near the rear of the unit with about 10 brothers sitting around it engulfed in heavy conversation. Dog walked away thinking to himself, "I knew it was something about shorty that I liked, he's a Muslim, he's laid back, he's going to be alright. He don't even look like the type that be getting in trouble on the streets. He probably was getting a little money doing hand to hand and made a sale to an undercover. Word!" Dog shook the thought off and kept it moving.

Tone finished up then walked out to find the phone. Tone said to himself, "I hope these Niggaz don't get it twisted because I got the lil baby face. Dudes are always judging a book by its cover. Niggaz gon find out."

One phone was free so Tone tried the access numbers he was given in R&D which allows him to process his phone calls. The numbers weren't working so he retreated to the Bubble to ask the C.O. for assistance. He looked at the nametag on the officer's chest, it read "Dunlap."

"Excuse me, Ms. Dunlap," said Tone.

"Yeah, may I help you," said Ms. Dunlap in a voice that in six months would sound like the sexiest voice in the world to Tone.

"Yeah, I'm trying to call my people, but the phone is saying that I'm already in use or something. How long will it be before my numbers begin working?" Said Tone observing his I.D. card.

"I just put them in Mr. Wheeler. Try them now."

When Tone turned around, he noticed a dark skinned fella about 5'9", 210 pounds, leaving the phone, but the phone was off the hook like the guy was about to use it.

"Ayo Black," screamed Tone. "Yo Black," he continued.

The guy turned around.

"Ayo Black, are you about to use the phone because I just tried my numbers and they didn't work a second ago, but now I'd like to try them again," yelled Tone. They guy walked toward Tone and began to speak.

"Ayo, my name is Diamond dog. I run the phone in here. The one the blacks use at least. Each phone is for somebody. The whites have theirs, the Chinese be calling their restaurants and shit all day, the Spanish got their San Juan joint, and we have ours."

Folding his arms and grabbing his chin, Tone replied with, "I'm saying, what do you mean you run the black phone? I don't understand. What, I have to ask you if I want to call my mom or something? I thought it's whomever goes hard, they use it. What the fuck yo! I'm not ass," said Tone firmly.

Diamond chuckled to himself and said, "Nobody said you were ass, but this isn't Riker's Island either youngin. This is the Feds homey. Shit is different in here. All this phone shit is collect and prepaid, and you can't ride it either. Fifteen minutes, then your shit cuts off. Then you have to wait an hour before you're able to call again. Now first of all, I don't boguard the phones or nothing like that. I've just been here the longest so I keep things sensible. Dudes be fucking up the lines for the phone and people be losing their spots so I keep the order. That's all black man. But listen here, don't get it twisted. Just because dudes aren't on no rah rah shit, don't think that it can't happen. Or that it won't. But like I said, I just keep the order homeboy. Just let me know when you need to use it and I got you. Ah-ight! We cool?" said Diamond extending his hand.

Responding Tone said, "Yeah, I got you. No doubt. Hey, where are you from anyway?"

"I'm from Detroit. Rock City."

"What the hell are you doing in New York?"

"I was taking care of some business, and having fun at the same time and something jumped off. It just so happen to jump off while I was here in New York near it. I didn't do anything though, which is why I'm on trial now. But holla at me though."

"What do they call you youngin?" he added.

"Tone. They call me Tone, or Tony. Or Ock."

"Yo, you know," said Diamond as Tone interrupted.

"Yeah, they're over there. I know. Good looking though. Just let me use the phone after you so I can see if my shit is working yet."

"Go head Tone, use it now. Shit, you just coming in. Handle your business," said Diamond finally able to go and use the restroom.

Tone raced back to the phone and tried his numbers once again, this time he was successful. Tone heard a few clicks, then a message was heard, "Please say your name at the tone." Tone cleared his throat and waited for the tone. "Tone!" he yelled. "Thank you," replied the computer. After a few more clicking noises, Tone heard the phone ringing. After two rings, Tone heard Tonia say, "Hell," but she was quickly cut off by the recording. "This is a VAC collect call from an inmate at a correctional facility. This call is from 'Tone.' If you would like to accept the call, press '5' now. If you would like," but before the recording could end, Tonia pressed '5' and the call went through.

Beeep!

"Hello," said Tone.

"Hey Pa, how are you? Are you okay in there?" asked Tonia. She began to cry.

"I'm alright Ma. Stop crying, please. I need you to be strong Ma. You have to hold it down for real now Ma. Stop crying."

"I know Pa, I can't," Her crying increased, "they killed Dev. Why? I was so scared. I thought we lost you too," she added.

"No Ma, your Boo is ah-ight. But check it though, I'm not really trying to talk too much over this phone. The guy who processed me told me that immediate family and a girlfriend didn't need to have a visiting form filled out. I put you down as my common-law wife anyway when I filled out the papers, so basically you're good."

"When can I come Pa?"

"Come tomorrow around 2 o'clock, alright?"

"Okay Pa."

"But besides that, how are you doing?"

Tonia sniffled a little bit then she responded, "It's crazy out here Pa. Everybody is running around here saying all kinds of shit talking about how y'all killed Black."

Tone immediately cut her off. "Ma, didn't I just say to watch what you say on these phones? Listen, I had money in my pocket when I got arrested so I'm good for now on that tip. Plus, I can't have any packages sent in here. I have to buy everything from off of the commissary. I also think it'll be best if you stayed at your mother's house for a while. Besides, them people are probably going to be tailing you and all that. Just chill out, go to work and come home and wait for my phone calls. Alright? And keep your eyes and ears open. I'll see you tomorrow. Yo Ti Quero Mucho!" said Tone telling Tonia that he loved her.

"Yo Ti Quero Tambien," she replied telling him she loved him too.

Tone headed into a realm of his new world as Tonia, on the other side of the city, buried her face into her pillow and cried herself to sleep. Tone headed back to his cell and fell asleep thinking about who it could be that was snitching on him. Could it be Basehead Dave or Eugene's sorry ass. Tone always knew never to leave loose ends. Apparently he has. Too late now though. Any and everybody's a potential witness to him.

CHAPTER THIRTY

"Chow," yelled a big black guy that everyone called Big Abdullah. He stood behind a food cart placing hot oatmeal and two pieces of toast on every inmate's tray. It was 6 A.M. and inmates began filing out of their cells, one, two at a time forming a line to get their food. After breakfast was served, some people returned to their bunks and some remained outside of their cells. Tone took a shower and contemplated his next move. He decided to take a nap and after lunch was served, went through the same procedures he did at breakfast time, he sat back now waiting for his visit.

"Wheeler! Anthony Wheeler! Visit!" said a female C.O. who was walking around in the unit making sure everyone was okay. The rear end on this woman would make any man drool. She already looked good to Tone, and Tone just got arrested the day before. He imagined how the other inmates like Junior, Dog and Diamond viewed this woman. She probably looked like Janet Jackson to them.

"Here I go miss," said Tone walking toward the lady.

Stopping and placing her hand on her hip, the C.O. responded by saying, "Who are you?"

"I'm Wheeler. You called me for a visit," said Tone placing his hands behind his back.

"Didn't you just get here yesterday?" she asked.

"Yes ma'am."

"Damn, it usually takes a week or so before people start getting visits. Let me find out," said the C.O. with a small smile on her face. Tone waited for his pass that would allow him access to roam freely throughout the building and looked at the officer's nametag. It read "McCoy." Ms. McCoy gave him the pass.

"You enjoy your visit Wheeler."

"Thank you Ms. McCoy," said Tone dashing off to his visit.

Ms. McCoy watched Tone as he left for his visit and thought to herself, "Damn, he's cute and he's polite."

After a two-hour visit with Tonia and Tone's mom, Tone returned to his unit to finally get settled in. Everything hadn't hit him yet, but he knew that he was in for the long haul. As soon as he returned from his visit, he headed into one of the small T.V. rooms. He noticed an empty seat and walked over to it hoping to accompany the group that was watching the latest and greatest in music videos.

"Ayo money," said a voice from behind Tone. Tone ignored it. "Ayo money, somebody got that seat already." Tone turned around and realized that it was a heavyset black dude that he saw working out yesterday. The guys in there called him Kendu.

"Is he coming right back?" asked Tone.

"It don't matter. That's his seat," said Kendu with an attitude.

"Yeah, you're right. I respect that." Tone stood up and picked the chair up with him and tossed it at Kendu hitting him square in the face with it. "Fuck your man! Fuck you, and fuck this chair! I go hard nigga! I ain't ever going home! I don't give a fuck about nothing and none of you dudes in here. Whatever! We can go!" said Tone looking crazy in the face now. Usually when a scene like this jumps off, dudes know something is not right with the guy. People know when to fall back, and when a dude is faking. Right then, Tone was not faking. Another kid they called Nitty moved his chair a little bit for whatever reason.

"Ga head nigga! Jump! Pop off! I'll turn your bitch ass into a pizza when I'm done slicing your faggot ass up. You think I give a fuck about y'all dudes in here. What!" Said Tone looking around.

Kendu was on some workout shit hard so he figured all his working out had to pay off. He got up and charged Tone. Tone grabbed Kendu and slammed him on the floor as the occupants gave the fighters room to thump. Tone had Kendu on the floor, leaning over him swinging at everything that was exposed. "You fucking Brooklyn ass nigga! I ain't never liked y'all grimy ass niggaz anyway! Always trying to take somebody's shit! Well take this you mafuckin bitch ass nigga! Fight back you bitch! I'll kill your fucking ass in here," he yelled as he continued to pound Kendu unconscious and back to consciousness again and again. The Muslims came running in.

"Asalamulaikum Ock! Asalamulaikum! Ock! Ock! Asalamulaikum!" yelled the Muslim brothers trying to pull Tone off the delirious and suffering Kendu.

"Watch out Ock! I got him!" said Big Abdullah who stood 6'9", 275 pounds, all muscle. "Asalamulaikum Ock!" shouted Big Abdullah.

Tone didn't respond. Big Abdullah grabbed Tone by his waist and picked him up over everyone and carried him out of the T.V. room. Abdullah looked Tone in the face. "Asalamulaikum Ock!"

"Walaikumasalaam!" said Tone a bit calmer now, but still ready for war. Tone began pulling on his clothes, adjusting them back to their normal fit.

"Ock, you're a Muslim right?" asked Big Abdullah.

"Yeah Ock," said Tone walking away. Abdullah reached for Tone.

"Come here Ock. Let me holla at you. Ock, be humble. Be humble Ock. What's the matter with you? You just got in here. This ain't Riker's Island."

"Well I'm not pussy either. And I definitely ain't no game so niggas better not try to play me," said Tone thinking out loud.

"Is everything alright?" asked Kalid, another Muslim brother who Tone later found out was from Webster Avenue in the Bronx.

"Yeah, he's alright," said Big Abdullah.

"Excuse me fellas, is everything alright around here?" asked Tim. Tim was an older Christian brother who understood and respected all religions and cultures, but had a special connection with the Muslims.

"Yes my good brother," said Big Abdullah.

"Well I'm here if y'all need me."

"Thank you Brother Tim." Abdullah nodded and Tim walked away.

"Ockie, what is your attribute?" asked Big Abdullah.

Tone had his arms crossed.

"Sabur!" Pronounced Sah-Bore.

"And what does that mean Ockie?" asked Abdullah trying to make a point.

"Patience, why?"

"Be patient then Ock!" Abdullah walked Tone over to his own cell and the two of them talked inside for about a half an hour. Abdullah let Tone go to get himself together and let him know, since he's the block Adaba, which is the Imam or the head Muslim of the unit, that Tone must respect him. Tone agreed and then walked away to his cell. As he was walking away, he let Abdullah know that he was serious by asking him to holla at him when it was time to offer their next prayer. People outside of the T.V. room heard the commotion and slowly gathered around mumbling words, sneaking glances at Tone as he walked to his cell. Tone's celly Junior heard about what happened after returning from a doctor's call-out and ran to his cell to see if Tone was okay.

"What appened Tone? Ya alright mon?" asked June.

"Yeah, I'm good," said Tone as he broke the plastic blade guard off his shaving razor.

"What ya doing yoot? Ya crazee mon?"

"Ayo check it son, dudes in here don't know me. Y'all don't know my case, or what the fuck is going through my head. I got a fucking body case, my mafuckin man died in my arms when I got arrested, my wifey is pregnant, my other man is on the run. You think I'm a let a mafucker in here play me? Some soft ass hot niggaz at that. Oh we're going to see about that! I will cut a niggaz' ass everyday if I have to. Fuck these niggaz! You see dudes be jumping out there and they don't even be realizing the repercussions to shit. Like me, I know, if I hit somebody up, I can catch a new charge. I already know this. I also know not to disrespect somebody, or anybody for that matter, especially if I don't know them because a nigga could have the same mentality that I have and fuck around and catch me off guard and really hurt me. But like I said, I'm trained to go. My guns ain't got no safety on them, in jail or in the streets. I got a possible death penalty case so I'm ready for whatever. But those little defaced serial number on pistol case mafuckas and those credit card white collar crime cats that ain't never been through the drama, myself, and a lot of other niggaz like me got a surprise for their ass," said Tone as he walked out of the cell.

"Chill out son," said Dog as he stopped Tone at his cell

door. "These dudes in here are ass. These dudes don't want no drama Tone. I told you that already. Be easy son. Fuck these dudes! Do you. It ain't worth it!"

"Well fuck it, I'm a go outside and chill. A nigga look at me wrong, he's gonna get it. Fuck that. I'm from the Boogie Down, and the Bronx don't breed no faggots." Tone got Dog looking at him like he was crazy. He just said to himself the other day that this guy looked like he was a humble dude.

"Just chill out mon," said June realizing that he should let Tone be to himself.

Ms. McCoy returned from her lunch break and got on the P.A. system. "Anthony Wheeler! Wheeler! Come up to the Bubble, now!"

Tone tucked the razor and headed to the Bubble. "Yeah, what's up?" He asked.

"Step outside, now," said Ms. McCoy as she buzzed the front door so that Tone could exit.

"What the hell is all this?" asked Ms. McCoy holding up a bunch of papers. "Do you know what this is Wheeler? These are slips just dropped saying you're in here on some gang stuff starting trouble. Now I've been working this house for three years now and we haven't been having any trouble and we're not going to start now. Now do I have to move you?" She rested her weight to one side and popped her gum as she chewed.

Tone lowered his head "No Ms. McCoy, I'm alright. I was just upset about a phone call and I started yelling. I'm cool now. It won't happen again. I promise. I like it here. And one more thing, I'm not a gang member, I'm a Muslim. Renegade Ock. Ya heard," he said smiling.

"Well whatever you are, there isn't going to be any renegading while I'm here and I don't want to hear anything else or you're out of here. Are we clear?"

Tone nodded in agreement and walked back to his cell thinking, "Damn, two more years around these clown ass dudes."

CHAPTER THIRTY-ONE

Two months after Tone's arrest …
Wednesday afternoon 1:30 p.m.

"**W**heeler! Visit!" yelled Ms. Dunlap.

"Tone! Tony! Sabur!" yelled Kalid, the good Muslim brother. He was cruising the Housing Unit looking for Tone.

Kalid peeked into one of the T.V. rooms. "Has anyone seen Tone?" He asked.

"He's in his cell, he might be praying," said Big Abdullah looking up from an intense game of chess.

Kalid went over to Tone's cell and saw Tone through the cell window finishing up his prayer. Tone was in his final sitting position, also called Jalsa in Arabic, and first turned his head to his right looking over his shoulder. He mumbled the words, "Asalamulaikum Warahmatullah!" He then turned to his left and said, "Asalamulaikum Warahmatullah!" Before Tone could continue seeking extra blessings through extended prayer called supplication, he noticed Kalid at his cell window smiling.

"Asalamulaikum Ock!" said Kalid smiling.

"Walaikum Asalaam," replied Tone as he greeted his religious brother, saying may peace be upon him as well. "What's up Kalid?"

"They called you for a visit,".

Tone smiled. "When?"

"Just now."

"Alright, good looking out," said Tone as Kalid opened the door knocking at the same time.

"You may as well come in now Kalid. You're already halfway inside." Tone was folding up his prayer rug.

"I know, but a good Muslim is one who asks his brother for permission to enter his domain." Kalid was inside Tone's cell looking down at the photo's he had sprawled on his bed

Tone smiled again. "You're absolutely right, and I give you permission."

"Do you need any smell good oil?"

Tone pointed to his windowsill "Nah, I have some Blue Nile that I bought from the commissary."

"Do you ever wear Frankincense?" asked Kalid.

"Not often. I'm usually wearing Blue Nile. Wifey likes the way it smells," said Tone applying small amounts of Blue Nile to his neck and chin hairs.

"Are you in love Ock? Because all you ever talk about is Tonia."

Tone grabbed a photo of Tonia that was in a picture frame made from empty cigarette packs and stared at it.

"I love her to death Kalid. She's my heart for real."

"So why aren't you guys married?"

Tone put the picture frame on his desk

"She don't need a ring to be my wife. Just be there for me."

Kalid waved his hand telling Tone to quit the games and he took a seat on Tone's bed.

"Not right now with that rap stuff Tone. I'm for real. Y'all need to be married."

"You're right Kalid. Insha Allah, if Allah wills, we will be one day." Tone sat down beside him.

"Wheeler! Your people are going to leave if you don't hurry up," said Ms. Dunlap over the P.A. system.

"I'm coming!" He yelled.

"Yo, I'll holla at you later Tone. Enjoy your visit."

Kalid got up, gave Tone the muslim salutation and left the cell.

"No doubt," said Tone leaving for his visit.

Tone gets to his visit a few minutes later...

"Hey Pa," said Tonia kissing Tone hard with her tongue.

"I missed you," said Tone embracing his girlfriend.

"I missed you too Poppi," Tonia was staring at his eyes.

"I love you," Tone returned the gaze.

"I love you more." Said Tonia cordially.

Looking down at her feet, Tone said, "Damn Ma, what kind of shoes are those?"

Lifting her foot, Tonia replied with, "You like them Pa?"

He shook his head. "Yeah, they're nice."

"They're Nine West." She added.

Tone squinched his face up.

"What the hell is Nine West?"

"It's a shoe store for women. Do you like the way my hair is done?" she said turning her head from side to side.

"Hell yeah, you always keep yourself looking good Ma."

"So why you don't always tell me then?" Said Tonia blushing.

"I do."

In a whiny voice, she replied.

"No you don't."

Clutching her hand, Tone said, "Okay. I will for now on. I promise. But I shouldn't have to tell you. You already know you're a dime. I just wish I could be with you right now," said Tone pouting.

"You will Pa. Soon." She patted Tone's hand.

"Ma."

"Yes."

"Do you really love me?" said Tone looking at Tonia seductively.

"Of course Anthony, why?" She moved her seat closer to him.

"Marry me then."

Tonia lowered her neck, looked around and said,

"What?"

"Marry me. Why'd you say 'What' like that? All stink and stuff." Said Tone sitting up in his seat.

Tonia grabbed his hand again and said "I didn't. I'm just surprised. I know how you talked about not getting married in jail because you didn't want to make it seem like you were tying me down."

"I don't want it to seem that way.

"You're not Tony. Listen to me. When I told you that I'd only been with one other guy, one time, when I was 13, it was the truth. After I realized I made a mistake trying to be grown too fast, I said to myself, 'The next man I have sex with, I'll be in love with him and he'll be my husband.' Tony, I love you more than I think I love myself. Sometimes you think I'm stupid, but I'm not. When I heard about Beissy's mom getting shot, I put two and two together because Juanita hasn't been calling the house. Even though two wrongs don't make a right, I didn't say anything because you do you the way you do you I guess. But I knew."

"I don't know what you're talking about," said Tone convincingly.

"Whatever. But do you think I would've been staying at our home with all of that damn stuff in it, in my name at that, if I didn't love you? I would die for you Tony," said Tonia beginning to cry softly. "I would actually give my life to save yours because I couldn't live without you. I know you're strong. You can hold it down. Shit, I think you can stand anything. I can't! Once I gave my heart to you, that was it. No one else is entitled to this ass, and no one is entitled to my heart except our children. No one! So those rings you got in your safe, I'm putting mine on as soon as I go out to Jersey." Tonia gave Tone a look that said, "yeah nigga, I'm wifey for real now."

"What! What rings! How the hell do you know what's in my safe?"

"Don't worry about it, it's a wifey thing," said Tonia smiling.

"Nah, seriously, I usually don't slip. How do you know what's in my safe?" asked Tone moving closer to Tonia.

"All I have to say is just because our lovemaking puts me on cloud nine, don't think I always be asleep afterwards. I sometime be just chilling. Plus I had to make sure no other bitch had you living a double life." She rolled her eyes.

"You're crazy Tonia. That's why I love you so much." Tone gently pinched her cheek.

"Yup. That's right."

"So listen, I'll set up a ceremony in here and you just make sure that you get the marriage license."

"Been there. Done that."

"What! Since when?" said Tone blushing.

"Since I found out your son is going to be a big brother," said Tonia smiling.

"For real? When? I mean I had a feeling, but I wasn't sure."

"I don't know exactly Pa, but I know I'm 10 weeks."

"Damn, I can't even be there for my little Queen." Tone instinctively rubbed Tonia's stomach.

"What little Queen?" said Tonia twisting up her face.

"We better have a little girl. I already got one bad ass little boy."

"Yeah, well I want a boy myself."

"You want a boy, I want a girl. As long as I have the both of you, its all praises from Allah," said Tone caressing Tonia's cheek.

She smiled "That's right."

"Wheeler! Two more minutes!" said the visiting room officer.

"Damn that was quick honey," said Tonia.

"Time flies when you're having fun Ma."

"You can say that again," said Tonia as they both got up to embrace one another.

"I love you Ma."

"I love you too. And oh, I sent some more pictures Tone."

"Thank you Tonia. That's 500 and whatever you sent this time."

"Shut up. You act like you don't want my photos or something."

"I do Tonia. I love them. I'll call you when I figure you got home. Okay?"

"Okay. I love you," said Tonia blowing Tone a kiss.

"Love you too," said Tone as they both left the visit feeling like newlyweds.

CHAPTER THIRTY-TWO

Four months after Tone's arrest...

"Lopez!" shouted Ms. McCoy handing out mail. "Reid! Cogley! Johnson! Thomas! Wheeler!"

"Damn, I hope this is my Discovery papers," said Tone to Kalid as Ms. McCoy handed Tone a large yellow manila envelope.

"Who's it from?" asked Kalid.

Tone looked at the return address.

"Oh yeah, this is it. It's from my lawyer. Now I can find out who's snitching on me," said Tone walking to his cell with his mail.

"Jones!" Ms. McCoy continued. "Gay! Williams! Lopez! Lopez again. And Wheeler again!"

"Yo Tone! You got another piece. I got you," yelled Kalid. Kalid took the second piece of mail and brought it Tone.

"Oh, this is some more pictures and 'I miss you' cards from wifey," said Tone still concerned more about his court papers. Tone opened Tonia's envelope and saw about 40 pictures of her at home showing her stomach and her at work filling prescriptions. There was a short letter inside. It read:

"Dear Husband of Mine,

I miss you! I love you! I can't wait to see you again on your next visit! Everybody asked about you. My mom and Michelle say hi. XOXOXOXOXOXOXOXOXOXOXOXOXOX!

Love, Your Wife …

P.S. Enjoy the photos."

Tone put the photos away in another large envelope with all the other photos he had gotten already. He then opened the envelope addressed from his attorney. Inside were five witness statements … He read them carefully.

DD5 INCIDENT REPORT: SHOOTING

DATE OF REPORT: 3/5/95

NAME:

TIME: 10:20 P.M. LOCATION: PSA 8 HOUSING PROJECT

I was looking out of my window and I noticed a group of guys standing in a circle. Approximately four male blacks, medium builds, with dark colored clothing. I left the window to use the bathroom and I hear five or six gunshots. I run back to the window and I see the victim on the floor. I dial 911 and explain to the operator what just happened and to send help. I then run downstairs to aid the victim who was bleeding profusely from the head and face but I noticed that he was still breathing. I tried talking to him and I asked him who shot him. He never replied. The police and the ambulance came. They told everyone to back up. Then they started asking questions.

OFFICER: JOHN HENRY

2

DD5 INCIDENT REPORT: HOMICIDE

DATE OF REPORT: 3/6/95

NAME: DR. PATRICIA LOPEZ

<u>TIME: 1:37 P.M. LOCATION: BX MED EXAMINER OFFICE</u>

At approximately 11:00 p.m., 3/5/95, a male black appx. 6 ft. 190 lbs. was listed as a John Doe. At 1:37 p.m. on 3/6/95, John Doe was tentatively identified by a relative as Antron Little. Shot twice in the mouth, and three times above eyebrows.

OFFICIAL: DR. PATRICIA LOPEZ

3

DD5 INCIDENT REPORT: SHOOTING

DATE OF REPORT: 3/5/95

NAME: DR. PETER STONE

TIME: APPX. 10:07 P.M. LOCATION: O.L.M. HOSPITAL

At appx. 9:34 p.m., we were dispatched from control to respond to a shooting of a male located at 1187 E. 226th Dr. We immediately headed for said location and upon arrival, met with crime scene officer's keeping people away from the victim. We noticed the victim was still breathing so we set up I.V. and Oxygen for the victim. Placed him on medical bed and proceeded to Our Lady of Mercy Medical Center. By the time we arrived the victim was D.O.A.

OFFICIAL: DR. PETER STONE

4

DD5 INCIDENT REPORT: HOMICIDE

DATE OF REPORT: 4/8/95

NAME:

TIME: 1:31 P.M. LOCATION: PSA HOMICIDE OFFICE

On March 5, 1995, I was looking out of my window and I saw a guy I know from the neighborhood standing in a group with three or four other guys. XXXXXXXXXXXXXX walks up and the guy I know as Anthony Wheeler pulled out a gun and shot Antron 6 times in the face. Anthony then ran up the block and disappeared.

OFFICIAL: FBI Agent Roberto Delano

5

DD5 INCIDENT REPORT: HOMICIDE

DATE OF REPORT: 3/5/95

NAME: OFFICER JOHN HENRY

TIME: 10:29 P.M. LOCATION: PSA HOUSING AUTHORITY

At appx. 9:36 p.m. my partner, Bill Tate, and I responded to a 187, a shooting. We were dispatched to a location known for drugs and responded thereafter. Upon arrival we noticed what appeared to be a black male, lying on the ground with multiple gunshot wounds to his face. Noticing he was still breathing, we radioed in to O.L.M. Med. Center and were told that a unit was on its way. We then sealed off the area with yellow tape. When back up arrived, we began canvassing the area for witnesses.

OFFICIAL: OFFICER JOHN HENRY

CHAPTER THIRTY-THREE

One year later…

Everything was in order. Tonia had given birth to a beautiful baby girl that they named Devina in memory of Tone's best friend Devin, since Tone wanted to always have Dev close to him. Tonia had also been coming through with the visits on a regular basis, and Slick was still hiding out somewhere. No one knew who the snitch was yet, and Tone had gotten into full bid mode now.

"Ms. McCoy, what's popping Ma," said Tone flirting with the C.O.

"Isn't that what you call that girl that you be talking to on the phone?" said Ms. McCoy strolling through the unit.

"Yeah, and …" Tone strolled beside her.

"You better stop before she finds out and comes over here and kicks your ass. Plus, I thought you were going home soon. What happened? Why are they still keeping you here?" asked Ms. McCoy stopping near the water fountain.

"I have a murder case Ms. McCoy. I thought you knew

that. Don't you C.O.s have computers and stuff that gives you all access to our files and records?"

"Yeah, but we're not allowed to look at you guys charges because if somebody's a snitch and other people find out, it isn't supposed to be able to come from us."

"I understand. But hopefully something will happen real soon with me. I'm going to trial with this one. I'm a gambler. I have to go since it's Federal. If I blow, I'm dead. They're giving me the needle. And if I cop out, I'm dead. Natural life! But if I beat it, my whole life is going to change. Especially since I've been on my deen and praying and everything everyday like I'm supposed to. It's hard sometimes, but I do my best. You see, my religion is easy, it's people that make it hard."

"Well you seem like a well-rounded positive individual Wheeler. You need to be home, with your handsome self," said Ms. McCoy making Tone blush from ear to ear. Tone's a playboy, Ms. McCoy should never have told him that.

For the next couple of weeks, Tone played Ms. McCoy extremely close. He figured, if he could get her, no telling what he could get out of her. In the middle of the third week, Ms. McCoy comfortable now, finally cracked.

Ms. McCoy and Tone were in the officer's station having a conversation. "I'm saying Ms. McCoy, you're trying to tell me, if I went home tomorrow, found out where in Queens you lived, left 12 dozen roses at your doorstep, yellow pedals at that, with a note from me along with my phone number on it, you wouldn't call me to thank me?" asked Tone looking directly into Ms. McCoy's eyes.

"Maybe," said Ms. McCoy blushing. Ms. McCoy had lately been wearing extra tight pants to work, more perfume, and always asking Tone to clean the officer's station while everyone else went to work and recreation.

Tone sat down beside Ms. McCoy.

"Let me ask you a personal question Ms. McCoy."

"Go head," she said blushing.

"First of all, how old are you?" he asked.

"I'm 25, and you?" She said while flirtingly rolling her eyes.

"I just turned 24. And, this isn't about me. It's about you sexy."

"Okay, go head," said Ms. McCoy sounding sexier than ever.

"It's a freaky sexual question so don't get mad and pull the pin on me," said Tone laughing.

"I won't."

"If I told you that I could eat you out and make you reach two orgasms in ten minutes, but I was on the streets saying this, would you allow me to prove it?"

"Nope. Cause you couldn't do it. Now help me with these supplies. I need to bring some more envelopes and pads out of the closet. You guys be writing all those dag on letters everyday. Y'all should be writing books." Said Ms. McCoy raising up from her sat.

"Inch be writing all the books with his crazy little ass," said Tone following Ms. McCoy to the supply room.

"I thought that he was going home soon too," she asked.

"I think he got a drug case, he's trying to go to trial too," said Tone locked on Ms. McCoy's rear end.

Earlier, when Ms. McCoy got out of her chair, Tone noticed that it looked to be damp or somewhat moist. He touched it and proved himself right, then proceeded with his game.

"Here Wheeler, take this," said Ms. McCoy pulling boxes from a shelf in the supply room. When Ms. McCoy turned to hand Tone a box, Tone kissed her on the lips. When she didn't respond by pulling the alarm button, Tone grabbed her by the back of her neck, pulled her closer to him and kissed her again, this time, with his tongue. He placed his hand on the crotch of her pants and heard her give off a soft moan. He realized how wet she was and figured this could be the chance of a lifetime. However, all that kept coming to his mind was Tonia, the love of his life, their beautiful daughter, how wifey was trooping the bid with him, and how she didn't deserve to be played. He pulled away from Ms. McCoy and said to her, "I'm sorry. I can't Ms. McCoy. You are too cool of a person. I really like you and would love to be with you, but I'm not single and I love my wifey to death. Plus, if you were my girl, I wouldn't do this to you neither. I know dudes that would kill for this opportunity, but I respect you as a black woman, you and my wife, more than anything. Let's just forget what just happened and continue being normal. Okay?" said Tone looking at her candidly.

"You know what Wheeler, you are so different from them other little nasty ass dudes in here that be jerking their stuff off at me. You never did that, and you always spoke to me with respect. I really respect you even more now. I even prayed for you last night. I really did. I hope things work out with your situation because your wife is a very lucky lady. You're a really good man too, I can tell. Now enough of the emotional stuff Mr. Carl Thomas," said Ms. McCoy as they both laughed. "Now finish bringing these boxes to the Bubble Wheeler." Ms. McCoy walked off smiling.

Tone helped her with the boxes feeling better than ever now because after being on dead time for over a year, he still felt that he had what it took to win over the ladies. That great personality that his woman loved him so much for.

CHAPTER THIRTY-FOUR

The date was May 1, 1997, almost two years after Tone's apprehension. He hadn't gotten any sleep because he'd been up all night praying. After about six months into his bid, Tone realized he needed to stop playing with God and get on his deen hard. Ever since that day, he'd been offering his five daily prayers regularly. After making his necessary phone calls that evening, he locked himself in his cell and stayed up remembering and praising Allah. Tone now sat in the holding cell in the Federal court building. In a moment, Tone will be escorted into the courtroom for trial. He has to enter before the jury arrives, because the seven man, five woman panel isn't supposed to know that Tone is currently incarcerated. The reason for that is to eliminate any bias that may enter into the jury's mind. Anyone of ignorance may assume because he's already in custody that perhaps he is guilty. The same court officers that were present at Tone's arraignment and all his other court appearances were also present on this fateful day.

All news media had been barred once again from the

courtroom to insure a fair trial and to avoid it from becoming a media circus. When Tone entered the courtroom, he noticed his friends and family who filled the rows behind the defense table. He also noticed the friends and family of the deceased, all seated behind the prosecution table which was also adjacent the jury box.

All of Tone's family was present except his two incarcerated brothers. Mrs. Wheeler, Juanita, Antoinette, both of Slick's baby's mothers, Frenchie, Tenequa, Tonia and their daughter Devina, all were seated in the second and third rows of the packed courtroom. In the fourth row, Michelle, Tonia's younger sister, sat among a slew of Tone's friends from his neighborhood including Beezo, Pepsi, Inf, Prince, Islam, Chuck, Jess, Moe and a few others.

"Hey Anthony," said Mr. Buckman shaking Tone's hand.

"Hey Mr. Buckman. How are you?" said Tone responding.

"Good. Good. Listen, this may be a simple trial, or it may turn into a circus. We'll see. But at this time, do you have any questions or concerns Anthony?" said Mr. Buckman sitting down beside Tone.

"No, I'm okay. I have faith in the Creator that he'll guide me through this. I always told myself, I'll get what I deserve. Everything else is up to Allah. It's in his hands now. I do, however, want to see this witness bad as a mafucka," said Tone.

"Well, we're lucky. Due to the inapprehension of your friend, this didn't become a conspiracy case. Plus they know they couldn't indict you on conspiracy charges because it was them who let your friend go in the first place. They would've had to answer to the family of Mr. Little, to their superiors and to the public. The lone count of murder in the first degree is all we have to beat, and we're home free. Okay. Sshh! Here comes the jury now."

The jury walked in quietly with their heads down. The seven man, five woman jury were of mixed races. Some were white, some were black, two were Spanish and one was Asian. They took their rehearsed seats and waited for the judge to give them instructions. The judge came from his chambers and headed toward the bench. Everyone had butterflies.

"All rise," said the bailiff. Everyone rose quietly. "You may be seated," he added. "The Honorable Judge John Fargus is present. Court is now in session."

For the next two hours, the judge instructed the jury on how they must decide the case. He emphasized that everyone must have an open mind, use rationale, and more importantly, use their common sense.

"Ms. Babara Judd, would you like to begin with your opening statements for the prosecution? Are you ready Ms. Judd?" asked the judge.

The prosecuting United States attorney in the case, Ms. Babara Judd, was a short dark skinned woman with short curly hair. She had a large butt with matching large legs. She also had 12 years experience working in the district attorney's department, and she hadn't lost a case in the last five years. Murder trials were also her forte.

"Ladies and gentlemen of the Court, I would like to take this opportunity to explain to you why a monster, this monster, Mr. Anthony Wheeler," said Ms. Judd now in Tone's face, "should pay for the death of an innocent man. Ladies and gentlemen, he should pay for this lost life, with his own in jail for the rest of his. Mr. Anthony Wheeler should be found guilty of murdering this son of a hardworking mother and once a future father. This man, this victim of Mr. Anthony Wheeler, was out one night, for whatever reason, but never returned home because a heartless, ruthless beast chose to take things into his own hands, like he's God Almighty, and take Mr. Little's life.

You'll hear testimony of how Mr. Anthony Wheeler took Mr. Little's life, and did so with no remorse. Ladies and gentlemen of the jury, I ask that at the end of this trial, upon hearing, listening to and evaluating all the evidence and facts, that you undoubtedly return a guilty verdict against Mr. Anthony Wheeler. Your Honor, that is all for now," said Ms. Judd firmly she then took a seat.

"Mr. Buckman, you may proceed," said the judge.

Mr. Buckman walked over to the jury box and scanned all the jurors. During jury selection, Mr. Buckman took note of who would seem convincing and easily influenced, and he remembered their names as part of his strategy. "Hello Ms. Martin," said Mr. Buckman to juror #2, a black simple woman, mother of an autistic son and crack addicted daughter from the Bronx.

"Hello Mr. Buckman, how are you?" she said grinning. He moved over and continued to scan the jury box until he locked his eyes on juror #7, a Puerto Rican man in his late 30s with craters on his face for using shaving razors without water. "Mr. Rodriguez, how are you doing this morning sir?"

"Oh, fine thank you," said Mr. Rodriguez with a smile.

Mr. Buckman moved back, scanned the courtroom, then returned his attention to the entire jury. "Good morning to you all!"

The entire jury replied in unison like school children greeting their teacher, "Good morning Mr. Buckman!"

"Well quite honestly, there is really no way to cut this. Unfortunately, a man, a son, as Ms. Judd well informed us, has lost his life. Nothing has been proven. No weapon has been recovered, and no motive has been established. But since my client is charged with this crime, I'm here to convince you, the jury, that if you have an open mind, and listen to all the evidence, analyze and evaluate it and more importantly use your common sense, that you will return a not guilty verdict against my client. Thank you ladies and gentlemen. Your Honor, that is all for now," said Mr. Buckman as he finished, he then proceeded back to the defense table.

"Mr. Buckman, tell Anthony that I'll be heading out to use the restroom," said Tonia.

"Okay Tonia," said Mr. Buckman. He relayed the message to Tone and Tonia headed out to relieve herself. Tonia walked toward the ladies room and an elevator that she had passed on her right opened. She heard a voice coming from the canveyor which was far too familiar to let pass. She made a U-turn and immediately spotted Eugene, Tone's brother, being escorted to an adjacent room next to the courtroom his trial was being held in. Tonia anxiously ran back into the crowded courtroom and signaled Mr. Buckman with a "psss, psss". Mr. Buckman turned around from discussing the case with Tone to see who it was that was causing the small commotion.

"Mr. Buckman! Mr. Buckman!" Tonia was shouting but whispering at the same time.

Mr. Buckman stood up and walked over to the door where Tonia was standing. He asked. "What is it Tonia?"

"I just seen Anthony's brother, Eugene, being escorted in handcuffs to a room right next door. Do you think he could be the witness?" she asked excitely.

"I don't know, let's see." Mr. Buckman dashed back over to Tone, leaned into him and whispered. "Anthony, Tonia said she just saw your brother, Eugene, being escorted into a room next door, perhaps an adjacent courtroom. Is it possible that your brother is the witness.

Shrugging his shoulder, Tone responded.

"I really don't know. I mean I have never discussed any of my business with my brother. We hardly even speak. I mean the last time me or my mom heard from him was when those Federal agents visited my mom at her house." Scratching his head, Tone continued "you know what, my mom probably told him that those feds came through looking for me and with the word already on the street, I know it could've flown through the jails like ducks fly south for the winter and some lucky snake could've picked up on it thinking it was a quick way out of doing jail time themselves". Tone sighed and said, "That mafucker! He and I had recently been beefing about some money, but I never thought his bitch ass would resort to this. Fuck him, he can't say shit about me, his ass has been in jail for the last two-and-a-half years," said Tone confidently.

Oblivious to Tones antics, the prosecutor was ready and motioned to the judge that she was ready to begin with her first witness. The judge nodded giving Ms. Judd the permission to proceed.

"Your Honor, the People would like to call their first witness to the stand. Medical Technician Peter Stone," said Ms. Judd confidently.

Mr. Buckman leaned close to Tone and said, "Anthony, the first few witnesses like the doctors, police officers, etc. are standard and routine. They really can't hurt us. It's the eyewitness that we have to worry about, okay? She's just putting on a show for now," said Mr. Buckman.

The medical Technician took a seat in the witness box as he had done so many times before.

"Mr. Stone, please state your full name and rank or position for the record," said Ms. Judd. Standing within a few feet of the witness.

"Paramedical Technician Peter Daniel Stone, Senior Ambulette driver for Our Lady of Mercy Medical Center." He smiled. Ms. Judd walked toward the jury booth.

"Mr. Stone, how many years have you been driving for the Our Lady of Mercy Medical Center?" She stopped and looked at him.

"Ten years ma'am." Said Mr. Stone with slight nod.

For the next forty-five minutes, Ms. Judd went through

a frivolous line of questioning with the medical technician, with crime scene officer, John Henry, and with the medical examiner, Ms. Patricia Lopez. Everyone basically told the same story that their records and statements had reported prior to the trial. Mr. Buckman then cross-examined each of the three witnesses simply for the sake of doing so. But when he cross-examined the medical examiner, Ms. Patricia Lopez, his strategy kicked in.

Mr. Buckman placed a pencil behind his ear, walked over to the witness, looked her in the eye and spoke.

"Ms. Lopez, you said that you have been in the medical field for 15 years and that you've been a practicing medical examiner for nine of those years, am I correct?"

"Yes sir." Said Ms. Lopez with a straight face.

"So is it fair to say that you're a professional in the medical field?"

"You can say that. Yes."

Mr. Buckman began walking toward the defense table.

"So Ms. Lopez, you testified earlier that Mr. Little was shot three times above the eyebrows. Is that correct?" He stopped and looked at a document he had at his table.

"Yes I did testify to that. They entered over the brow and exited the lower rear part of the cranium," said Ms. Lopez demonstrating on a chart which displayed a human skeleton for illustrative purposes. The chart was placed beside her on an easel.

"Ms. Lopez, my client is exactly 5'6. The victim, Mr. Little, was approximately 6'1, 6'2. Is it possible that the shooter in this case could've been someone taller than the victim?" he said approaching her slowly.

"Yes it's possible, Mr. Buckman, but…"

Mr. Buckman cut her off. "No further questions, Your Honor. You may excuse the witness," Mr. Buckman raced to his seat.

"Ms. Lopez, you may step down," said the bailiff.

Mr. Buckman's idea was to place into the jury's mind that another shooter may exist.

Ms. Judd returned to the floor.

"Your Honor, the People would like to call Professor Stan Riley of the New York City Forensics Laboratory at N.Y.U.," said Ms. Judd. The professor entered the courtroom and took a seat on the stand.

"You may proceed," said the judge.

"Professor Riley, if I may," said Ms. Judd asking him if it was okay to call him that. The professor nodded and Ms. Judd continued. "How many years have you worked in Forensics sir?"

The professor intertwined his fingers and answered her question. "While I was a student at N.Y.U. 13 years ago, I took an internship at the lab that I currently run. But it wasn't until two years after my internship that I became a certified Forensics Technician. After getting my degree in Criminal Science, I became an official employee of the New York City Forensics Specialists Unit."

"Is that where you're currently employed now Professor?" asked Ms. Judd pacing the courtroom.

"Yes ma'am, I am."

"So would you say you're an expert in forensics?" Asked Ms. Judd stopping and spinning around on one heel until she came face to face with her witness.

"Yes ma'am, I guess you can say that."

"You guess I can say you're an expert in forensics, or you are an expert in forensics?"

"I am an expert ma'am," said the professor sternly.

"When you were called in to give your analysis of this particular crime scene, what did you find?" Ms. Judd walked over to the prosecution table and began looking at one of her documents.

"Well at the New York City Forensics Specialists Unit, we're comprised of four teams with three people appointed to each team. I run all the teams, but I remain at headquarters unless I'm called in for something overwhelmingly out of the ordinary."

"Were you called to this particular crime scene?" She gave the professor a quick stare.

"Yes ma'am."

"And what made this crime so overwhelmingly out of the ordinary Professor?" said Ms. Judd shooting a glance at the jury.

"Well it was the type of bullets that were actually used. Black Talons are a black market bullet that only a few organizations can get their hands on. Unlike most bullets on the market today, Black Talons have a 99% fatality rate. So I was called in to investigate, to try and find a connection to something."

"Did you find anything Professor?" The Professor gave his attention to the jury.

"Nothing unusual really except that the distance from where the body was found and where the spent shells were located didn't coincide with the powder marks on the body that determine the proximity of the shooter."

"Does that normally occur Professor?" Ms. Judd shifted her gaze back to the jury.

"It doesn't normally, but it does occur."

"Thank you Your Honor, and thank you Professor". Ms. Judd nodded and smiled. "Mr. Buckman", she nodded again "your witness," said Ms. Judd quietly strolling over to the prosecution's table.

"Your Honor, may I?" asked Mr. Buckman getting up from the defense table.

"Sure," replied the judge.

Mr. Buckman leaned over to Tony for a few moments and then proceeded with his line of questioning. After about eight to 10 minutes, Mr. Buckman ended his cross-examination. However, during his line of questioning, Mr. Buckman emphasized the location of the spent shells. Strategy perhaps.

"Alright Ms. Judd, Mr. Buckman, it is understood that there is one witness left. Let's take a lunch recess and when we return, hopefully we can wrap this thing up. I know the jury is tired and worn out. I'd like to hope that everyone could bare with us for just a little longer," said the judge tapping his hammer. He then announced the lunch recess. Mr. Little's family exited and walked to a nearby diner; the family and friends of Tony remained seated. Everyone's appetite was replaced by butterflies because they knew the next and last witness would determine Tone's fate. After almost an hour and a half, the jury was ushered back into the courtroom and the Littles entered shortly thereafter.

Mr. Buckman and Tone sat calmly as if they knew the outcome of the case.

"All rise!" shouted the bailiff. Everyone rose. "You may be seated!" he added as the judge also took his seat.

"Your Honor, if it's alright with you, I'd like to begin," said Ms. Judd. Fumbling with her papers.

"You may proceed. Call your next witness." Said the judge.

"Your Honor, the People would like to call Ms. Latonya Little to the stand." Everyone looked around in amazement as Ms. Little entered from a rear door of the courtroom. She was casually dressed in a polyester skirt suit and as she walked toward the bench, she handed her jacket to a female who could either be the victim's sister, cousin, or girlfriend. "Ms. Little, would you place your left hand on the Bible and raise your right hand." Ms. Little complied and took her seat. "Do you swear to tell the truth, the whole truth, and nothing but the truth, so help you God?" Asked Ms. Judd.

"I do," replied Ms. Little.

Ms. Judd then proceeded.

"Ms. Latonya Little, I know this may be hard for you, but your testimony is important and crucial to the court. I'll need you to speak loud and clear into the microphone, okay?"

"Okay." Ms. little nodded.

"Ms. Little, will you tell the court your relationship to the victim." Ms. Judd stood very close to the witness' seat.

"Yes, I am Antron's mother," Said Ms Little. Her face seemed full of emotion as people in the courtroom begin making uncomfortable gestures.

"Ms. Little, on the night in question, will you tell the court where you were at approximately 9:30 p.m."

"I was at home looking out of my window." Ms. Little dabbed the corners of her eyes with a handkerchief.

"And where exactly is your home?"

"My home is at 1187 E. 226 Street Dr., in the Bronx."

"Is this where the shooting took place?" said Ms. Judd.

"Yes maam. My son died in my arms that night," said Ms. Little now crying as the jury focused all of their attention on her testimony.

"Ms. Little, would you like some water?" said Ms. Judd walking toward the prosecution table.

"Yes please." Ms Little's sobbing was coming under control.

Ms. Judd retrieved a bottle of Evian water and passed it to Ms. Little all while never taking her eyes off of the jurors.

"Ms. Little, would you please tell the court what it was that you saw happen to your son that evening."

"Well at about 9:30 p.m., I was waiting for Antron to come home. He had called me earlier that evening, so I was in my window watching out for him. While looking out of the window, I noticed four young men standing directly under my window having a conversation."

"How did you know they were having a conversation?"

Asked Ms. Judd.

"I could tell by how they were gesturing their bodies and turning around, back and forth, and also by seeing their mouths moving."

"So you couldn't hear them?" She took her position beside Ms. Little again.

"No, I couldn't."

"Continue Ms. Little."

"So I left the window, but I didn't really leave."

"What do you mean, you didn't really leave?"

"I ducked back out of sight from these young men because they kept staring at me. But I could still see outside."

"Then what?"

"Then I saw Antron walk up and began conversing wit the four guys."

"Then what happened?" Asked Ms. Judd being persistent.

"Then he began arguing with Mr. Wheeler over there," she said pointing at Tone.

"How did you know they were arguing?"

"Because Mr. Wheeler was looking in my direction. Antron had his back to me, but I could see all in Wheeler's face that it was an argument because he was showing his teeth in like a mad man's face. Like Aaarrghh!" said Ms. Little demonstrating.

A juror let out a small chuckle.

"Then the guy pulled out a black handgun and shot my son five times in the face."

"Is the shooter here today?" Ms. Judd confidently asked.

"Yes he is! He's sitting right over there with the grey suit on," said Ms. Little pointing toward Tone once again.

"Thank you Ms. Little. Wonderful job! No further questions Your Honor," said Ms. Judd. She smiled, walked over to her section and took a seat.

"Mr. Buckman, your witness," said the judge.

"Good afternoon Ms. Little," He said walking halfway toward the witness stand.

"Good afternoon sir," she replied.

"Ms. Little, what was the last grade that you completed in school?"

Ms. Judd stood up. "Objection Your Honor! This woman's educational history has nothing to do with this case!" She said angrily.

"Overruled! You may answer the question." Replied the judge.

"I'm currently enrolled at Bronx Community College. It's my senior year." Said Ms Little.

Mr. Buckman headed over to the defense table and picked up a piece of paper. He looked it over, then proceeded with his questioning. "Ms. Little, do you know what this is?" asked Mr. Buckman handing her a copy of her initial police statement. She looked over at Ms. Judd, received a nod, then looked back over at Mr. Buckman and answered.

"Yes."

"Can you read that for the court please," said Mr. Buckman turning and scanning the courtroom.

"Objection Your Honor, my client is in no clear state of mind to be reading anything!" interjected Ms. Judd, standing at the edge of her table.

"Overruled! You may read what it says," said the judge nodding at Ms. Little.

Ms. Little read her initial statement aloud dated 3/5/95.

"I was looking out of my window and I noticed a group of guys standing in a circle. Approximately four male blacks, medium builds, with dark colored clothing. I left the window to use the bathroom and I heard five or six gunshots. I ran back to the window and I saw the victim on the floor. I dialed 911 and explained to the operator what just happened and to send help. I then ran downstairs to aid the victim who was bleeding profusely from the head and face, but I noticed that he was still breathing. I tried talking to him and I asked him who shot him. He never replied. The police and the ambulance came. They told everyone to back up. Then they started asking questions."

Mr. Buckman continued with his strategy. "Ms. Little, earlier you stated a few things that contradict your previous testimony. You testified before that you never left the window, that you saw my client shoot your son, and that you asked your son, or the victim according to your statement, who shot him. Who did this? Isn't that what you told the police that night Ms. Little?"

"Yes but …"

"Ms. Little, if you saw my client, Mr. Wheeler, shoot your son, why would you have to ask your son 'Who did this? Who shot you?'"

"I wanted him to tell me! I wanted to be sure!" Ms Little was trembling.

"So you wanted to be sure Ms. Little."

"Yes, I wanted to be sure!" She shot a glance at Ms. Judd.

"You wanted to be sure because it wasn't clear to you what happened Ms. Little? You weren't sure who shot your son Ms. Little, is that right?"

She lowered her gaze. "No, I wasn't sure. But it was Anthony who shot my son!"

"Ms. Little, do you know what perjury is?" Asked Mr. Buckman walking over to the defense table.

"Objection Your Honor! Mr. Buckman is treating the witness like she's the defendant. The witness is not the one on trial here. Mr. Wheeler is!" said Ms. Judd again standing to her feet.

"Overruled! Ms. Judd, let Mr. Buckman finish his line

of questioning!" said the frustrated judge giving her a look that said "I'll hold you in contempt".

"Ms. Little," said Mr. Buckman walking over to the jury booth and looking at everyone as he spoke, "the prosecution previously brought to the stand a witness. Their witness, not mine. That witness testified to being a professional and an expert in his field and no one ever disputed that. So Ms. Little," said Mr. Buckman now looking every juror directly in the face, "when Professor Stan Riley testified that when a person is shooting an automatic handgun, that the shells are always spent to the right of the person, or behind them. You just testified that my client was facing in your direction and pointing the gun in your direction while firing. How is it scientifically possible then for the shells to have been spent to your right and not my client's right side as the diagram showed they were? And over eight feet to the right of the victim at that."

When Ms. Judd realized that the prosecution may have lost their case and that Ms. Little couldn't answer the question, Ms. Judd jumped up out of her seat and yelled, "Because they were running and probably kicked the damn shells to the other side!" demonstrating with a handful of pencils and almost falling doing so.

Mr. Buckman lowered his head and his voice. "Your Honor, I have no further questions. The Defense rests," said Mr. Buckman firmly as he walked back to his seat.

"Ms. Judd?" said the judge asking her without saying a word if she was finished.

"Your Honor, the People will not re-cross. We also rest our case," said Ms. Judd. Looking at Ms. Little.

"Closing arguments may begin when the People are ready," said the judge. "Ms. Little, you may step down."

Mr. Buckman pulled his seat up and leanded into Tone and said, "Anthony, how are you feeling?"

"Fine, you did great!" said Tone smiling.

"Well it's not over yet! The last advantage we have is that I get to close after Ms. Judd does and the jury remembers my words because I'm the last thing they hear."

Ms. Judd gave a 20-minute closing argument and tried to do her best by ending it with an emotional statement.

She stood still in front of the jury booth as she gave her speech.

"Ladies and gentlemen of the Court, Mr. Antron Little never asked for what happened to him on that fateful evening. Mr. Antron Little never wanted to abandon his mother. Mr. Antron Little never planned on leaving this world by gunfire. Mr. Anthony Wheeler made that choice for him! I ask that you come together collectively and return a guilty verdict against this monster. Thank you ladies and gentlemen, that is all," said Ms. Judd as she sat down at the prosecution table and began fiddling with papers that were lying scattered on the table.

Mr. Buckman took his position at the front of the courtroom and began to deliver his speech. He closed out sooner than the prosecution did and ended his argument simple.

"Ladies and gentlemen of the Court, use your common sense. Take into consideration everything that you've heard. Keep in mind any inconsistencies, any unreliable testimony, any unbelievable statements and anything you can't perceive from what you've just heard. I ask you today that because the People have not set forth a motive and have not produced a weapon therefore not proving their case beyond a reasonable doubt, that you 12 men and women of the jury return a verdict of not guilty. Remember, if anything that what you've heard makes you go 'Hhmmm!', then there's reasonable doubt and you must acquit. Thank you!" said Mr. Buckman as he silently returned to the defense table and took a seat next to Tone. The jury was then escorted into the jury room and people began to scramble for food, drinks, and the restrooms.

An hour later, a court officer screamed that the jury had

reached a verdict. Everyone returned to the courtroom and the jury entered while everyone was seated.

"Anthony, I'm nervous. I've never seen a verdict returned this soon. Remember, no matter what the outcome, be strong! I will not abandon you under any circumstances," said Mr. Buckman leaning over and speaking quietly to Tone.

Smiling, Tone replied with, "I appreciate everything you've done for me Mr. Buckman. I already told you beforehand, I'll get what I deserve. I am a firm believer in the Creator, Allah, and whatever was written out for me, must fall through. I will not question it either. Don't worry, I will remain strong until the day that I die," Tone seemed calmer than he'd been since the beginning of the trial.

"Have you reached a verdict yet Mr. Foreperson?" asked the judge.

The foreperson stood up. "Yes Your Honor!" replied a black heavyset man in his early 50s with pork chop sideburns. "We the People of the Northern District of New York have reached a verdict. We find the defendant, Mr. Anthony Wheeler, on the count of murder in the first degree, intentional murder, not guilty!" Antron's family bowed their heads in disbelief. Tone's family and friends were ecstatic. The judge excused the jury, and once the jury had exited the premises, Judge John Fargus headed for his chambers.

In an adjacent courtroom, Eugene was summoned to appear in front of a Federal judge to see if the Supreme Court would grant his motion, coincidentally on the same day as Tone's trial. Because it was Pro Se, Eugene had to appear in person. Unfortunately, his motion ended up being denied and Eugene was eventually sentenced to four to 12 years.

CHAPTER THIRTY-FIVE

One year after Tone was acquitted, he and Antonia were nestled away in their new oceanfront home, a quiet cul-de-sac located in the Hamptons section of Long Island. After the trial, the two decided that change would be healthy and the memories of their Teaneck residence weren't worth cherishing, so they moved back into New York. Tone's Real Estate investments earned him a ton of money. The properties he owned helped him maintain the lavish lifestyle that he became accustomed to. Now with over 4,600 square feet of luxurious living space the couple called their own, Antonia figured hiring an interior decorator was the best thing to do since buying her dream house. Built from the ground up, their elegant waterfront featured a family room with a 21-inch coffered ceiling, a magnificent rosewood floor, a large stone fireplace, and a fully equipped sit-down sunken wet bar complete with a classic mahogany finished bar top. The chef's kitchen with butler's pantry, a special request by Antonia to accommodate her with her exotic cooking, artfully merged marble, granite, and custom cabinetry with top of the line stainless steel appliances, and opened into a spacious dining room. A guest suite, game room, home gym and two additional bedrooms completed the first floor. A red oak stairway, Tone's choice, lead to the privacy of their master bedroom suite, which encompassed the entire second floor and was complimented by a library/study, a sitting room, and a 30' x 12' covered balcony overlooking their free-form heated pool that had "The World is Yours" engraved in its floor. Impact glass, a security system, 8 foot French doors and lush landscaping topped off their remarkable investment.

Clad in a white cotton tank top, white silk women's boxers and low cut socks with a colored ball attached to the rear of them to match the red barrette in her hair, Antonia emotionally expressed to Tone how the past few years had effected her.

The Mr. and Mrs. were in their bedroom watching television.

"Anthony," she empathetically began.

"Yes," said Tone as he got dressed putting on a white cotton crewneck T-shirt, a pair of light grey sweat pants and his favorite white on white Nike tennis shoes. Tone was standing up looking in his full length mirror while Tonia laid sprawled across their bed expressing her feelings to her husband.

"It's been a long time since I undertook what I knew was my destiny. I would love to say that the time you were away flew by, but you and I both know that time does what it does. I am definitely proud of you and the direction you chose to turn your life, our lives I should say. And if I had four quarters for every time that I asked Allah to hurry it up, I would've probably had all of this waiting for you when you stepped out of that jail cell. Sometimes I never thought this day would come, but here we are in the Hamptons," she said tearfully smiling, "with all of the drama behind us. We made it through countless V.I.s as you would call the visits, and those crazy phone calls," she said remembering all the senseless arguments they'd have over the phone with Tone always hanging up on her and calling her right back apologizing. "Anthony, I used to cry myself to sleep sometimes. Especially after receiving a letter from you or writing you one. Through that little bid, and now, I've been your best friend, your left titty," she said as he looked at her compassionately, "your secretary, accountant, therapist, mentor, sacrifice and excuse for many. Undeterred by it all, I've held my head and played my part as your wife. I am still able to say that through all the grief and sadness, I have no regrets Anthony. You always told me to lead and that you'd follow up. Well, I did my best. Now it's your turn to do you and drive this car. I've driven until I thought the wheels would fall off and never once did I think about abandoning ship. My only thoughts were to get out and push it. Now Pa, I'm ready to play my position next to you. Like a codefendant."

Tone was stunned. His wife's heartfelt words put him in a trance that kept him momentarily mesmerized until his beautiful daughter, Devina, began calling his name.

"Daddy. Daddy," she screamed playfully as she ran toward him dragging her feet and making her one-piece pajama suit sound like she had paper bags covering her toes. She reached Tone and jumped into his open arms and as cute as can be said to him, "Daddy, I wan go with choo."

Smiling at his adorable daughter, he looked at Tonia and said, "Ma, I'll be right back."

Tonia sucked her teeth and placed her hands on her head giving both Tone and Devina a look that said, "Oh no y'all didn't."

"Ma, she's so cute and irresistible. I promise, I'll be right back," said Tone kissing Devina over and over on her cheek.

"Well take Slick his dog. I'm tired of hearing his barking all day," said Tonia getting up from their bed.

Tone walked out the door and motioned Rocky, Slick's

tiger-striped pit bull, to hop in the back seat of his 1998 Cadillac Escalade, then he put Devina in the front seat and strapped her down. Slick continued dealing with the connect because everything seemed so sweet to him. He and Faye never reconciled their differences, and she went back to dancing. He still took care of his child that the two of them had together.

"I'll be right back Ma!" shouted Tone as he pulled off and headed to Slick and his new girlfriend's house in Jamaica Estates, Queens, to drop off Rocky to him. He popped in a CD and laughed at the words that suddenly blared from the speakers. "Oh you's a Muslim now/no more dope games…" a line from the late Great Tupac Shakur. A song he titled, 'I Ain't Mad At Ya!' Tone knew that Dev loved Tupac's music. He let the music play on and thought to himself, "Y'all can't be mad at me. I lived it, I loved it, I got lucky, and I left it. It's time to move on." Tone's cell phone rang.

Ring, Ring.

"Hello," said Tone. Tone put his phone on speaker and lowered the volume on his radio.

"Hey Tony, it's me Jonathan, your attorney."

Smiling, Tone said, "Aye John, what's up? Long time buddy."

"Yeah, sure is, about a year I guess. Hey, I got your postcard when you were in St. Tropez. I'm really proud of you and how you turned your life around Tony. You really impressed me and I admire that about you. I have to ask you something Anthony."

"Uh oh. Don't tell me that I still owe you some money."

"No, no, of course not. I want to know though, Tony, do you have any regrets about your life at all?"

Tone thought for a minute about his childhood, his sister Crystal, Beissy and her kids, his friend Dev, his children and the trial, but before he could answer, the beep in his car phone told him that someone was calling in on the other line. He snapped out of his momentary trance and said, "Hey Johnny."

"Yeah Anthony," replied Mr. Buckman.

"Hold on for a second, my other line."

"Okay."

Tone clicked over.

"Hello," said Tone calmly.

"Hey Pa," said Tonia.

"Oh, what up Ma?"

"Nothing, I just wanted to tell you that I love you! That's all."

"That's it?"

"Oh, and that I miss you very much too."

"I love you and miss you too Ma."

"Okay. Bye Pa."

"Bye Ma." Tone kissed her through the phone before he clicked back over to his lawyer.

"Mr. Buckman," said Tone deeply moved by his wife's remarks.

"Yeah Anthony?"

"I have none! Not one regret! And I'm grateful!"

"Okay then Tony, you take care of yourself and your family."

"You too Johnny. Holla…"

As soon as Tone hung up with his attorney, the phone began to ring again.

Ring! … Ring! … Ring!

"Yo," said Tone answering his phone.

"Son, I think you need to hear this," said Slick dramatically.

"Hear what? What's up?" Tone glanced over at his daughter.

"Yo … I just found out who killed your sister …"

THE END

FINAL WORDS! KEEPING IT GANGSTA!

Like the character 'Tone,' I've been through the rough city streets myself. From B-More to V.A., to South Cak and out to Ohio, it's real everywhere. Tone got lucky, but most of us don't. Try not to waste your time doing nothing. The physical life is short, accomplish something! Set a goal. Achieve it! Set a bigger one! When 9/11 happened, people around the world were devastated, but 9/11 happened for a lot of us 400 years ago. 9/11 happened when I lost my sister to the streets in '89. 9/11 happened to me when the system tried to lose me for the second time in May of 1997. 9/11 has happened to all of us one time or another. Let's get this clear into our heads, death is inevitable! It's in between that and birth that you must find out the reason that you are still breathing. I'm still searching. Maybe I've found out why but just haven't realized it yet. Brothers and sisters, if you have a God-given talent, use what he gave you. We only live once! And live not to regret it. Asalamulaikum!

ACKNOWLEDGEMENTS

Edenwald, we did it again baby! Holla!...

Crazy shout outs go out to all those who deserve it. If I forgot you and you are people, I still got love for you.

First and foremost I thank Allah the most high. Without the creator's blessing, none of this would be possible. Shout out to Ma- Dukes, Mrs. Sonja Thomas for putting up with me when I was in Tone's shoes. I love you mom. My sisters, Danita and Melissa, both of y'all inspire me. Rest in peace to my sister Crystal, this one's for you and Bo-Pete. We miss y'all. My brothers Big Frank and Ice. Wifey, Tania you are a blessing, a best friend, a co-worker and a terrific mother. Keep doing what you do. My son Jyamiene. I love you lil man and I got you in a minute. My princess Amiaya, without you, the company wouldn't have its name.

My Co-Dee's: Kevin (Buke) Gay, Delandro (Dee) Williams, Raphael (Swamp) Turrell, Abdul (Jar) Parmley, Jeff (Jus) Brown, Reginald (Koolaid) Jones

Edenwald: The Blue Park : Jesse, Jimmy, Lil Fred, my nephew Lil Frank, Cahiem, Calil, Lil Richie, Braindead, Jemel, Beissy, Charlene Dunlap, Ms. Holmes, Michelob, Nature, George McCoppin, Mario.

Trey Duece: Gerard (Shakim) Emptage, Brian (Beezo) Emptage, Artie (Choke No Joke) Alston, Kevin Smith, Bert Maxim, Islam Swift, Jermaine (Maine) Wiggins, Stephon and Mike Vernon, Antwan (Pretty Black) Vereen

1141: Enrique (Slick Rick The Ruler) Simmons, Ronald (The God Father) Simmons, Raymond (Big Ray) Simmons, Geto, Randy, Big B, Terrell, B.O., Terry (Box) Austin, Robot (R.I.P.) Austin, David and Chuck Williams, Unique and Robert Porter

1135: Lil Ron, Jemell (Casper) Hill, EZ

1160: Shawn (Billy The Kid) Turrell, Shawn (Bummy Shawn) Huggins, Kareem Huggins, Shawn Green, Shawn (Ramel) Baker, Tracy (Pop) Smith, Russell, Kim Cabble, Troy Cabble

1170: Damon (Yah Yah, Ski)Sumpter, Dion (Fly Guy) Sumpter, Monique Smart

1154:Devon (Mace R.I.P.) Calhoun, Huggie, Vincent (Valentine V.I.) Warren, Mrs. Burke, Fat Danny, Michelle, Michael Dawson, Tanya Fergerson, Annie

1159: Big Jus (Dustice)

The Line: Stephon (P.O.) Woffard

1173: Sharissa (Blow up Homie), Mary, Raquel and Freddy Castro, Lil Raven and Justine

1175: The Naked Faces, The Boxdales (Laura and Charlene), Cinammon, Ronnie& Pete

1161: Jeanette, Margie, Frances, Stacey, Tonya, Liza, Jael, Mikey, My Goddaughter Shaun. The Otano's

Bum Square: Fat Hasan, Tawanna, Ferdinand (Tuto) Rodriguez, Belinda, Cynthia, Joe-Joe (R.I.P)

The Horseshoe, Laconia Ave, Baychester Projects-Todd and Colby, The Valley- My Man Green Eyed Dee, 9 Finger Preme (Supreme)

The Green Family: Sabrina Green (R.I.P.), Daryl, (Imperial) Darnell (Downtown), Damon (Uptown), Jemel (Smelly), Troy (R.I.P), Jamilah. Devon (Kay Kay) Brown,

Gerald (Jaime-0) Jones, Ronnie and Carol, Raymond (Moe-Smash) Massey, Quentin (Tee) Dickerson, Quamay and Peanut, Marcus, Spofford, Antoine (A.C.) Cash, Big Earl, Lisa & Suyapa, Anthony (Prince) Parker, Andre (Dre) Smith, Kesha Shaw-Smith, Big Dawn Doctor, Alvin (True) Franklin, Trent (Bent) Hunter, Kevin Blackwood (R.I.P), Eugene (P.J.) (R.I.P.), Mongol and Fatshawn, Dula (Boston Secor), Don & Damon (R.I.P) Boston Secor, John (Rambo) Lyons-183rd, Prince Linton- Queens, Demetrius(Patience) Coppage- CT, Jeff (Dog) Taylor-118 South Jamica Queens, Lloyd (True)Stallworth-118 South Jamica Queens (True Wear coming soon), Eddie (DJ)Simms-Bx, Keith (Cash) McCrory-Harlem, Lawrence (Poncho) Washington, Pedro (Shorts) George- My old connect-The Bronx, Rock- Harlem, Smoke-Brownsville, Jermaine (Brazil) Johnson- Brooklyn, Malcolm (Black) Lassiter-NJ, Rosalyn (Poopie) Harper, Gab-Gacha-Corona Queens, Mentor (Albanian Ock), Dardani, Pervizaj-Queens, Lindsay (Jawad-Pepsi) Murray, Junior Black-Harlem, Eric Mobley, Shane (The Dribbling Machine) Mosley, Armando (Jab)Butler, David (Black-Buffalo) Thompson, Dylan Daniels-Bx, Omar and Mellow Kelsey-Philly, Patrick (Yusef) Britton, Francis (Junior) Brauner, Narvese, My Godson Louis and Isaiah Adorno, Evelyn-NC, Tanya-Bx,Danielle & Richard Krol, Tanya (Tiger-Bx), Steve (Apollo Pixel), Brian (B) Rowlette B-more, James (Jimmy Da Saint) Mathis-Philly, Shaun D. Brown-D.C., Antwan (Black Diamond) Kelso-Detroit, Razz-Bklyn, Tange-Columbus Ohio, Leyda Diaz-Bklyn, Evelyn Diaz-Bklyn, Allison Godfrey, Shaniqua & Latoya McCoy, the McCoy Family

Author's that showed love Moody Holiday ("Love's Twilight", "Wild Innocence a Tale from the Eighties" and

"Sweet Redemption"), Anthony Whyte ("Ghetto Girl's"), Mark Anthony ("Dogism"), Angela Wallace ("Secret Drama's")

To the people responsible for pushing my Books: My man CD-125th, A&B Books, Culture Plus Books, Baker and Taylor, Black Family Card (Bx), Nubian Hertiage (Harlem, Brooklyn and Queens), Hue-Man (125th), The IQ Spot (Manhattan), Black Star (Harlem 133rd Lenox), Harlem World Magazine, Black Horizon Book (Ryss), Major Book's Tri-State Mall (Delaware), Afrikan World Book (Baltimore Maryland), Waldens Book Store, Amazon.com, The Black Library.com, and Barnes and Noble.com

Oh yeah, big shout out to all of my people's in Columbus, Ohio, Keep doing what y'all do.

Holla at me!

Fan Mail Page

If you have any further questions, comments or concerns, kindly address your inquires in care of:

Antoine "Inch" Thomas

At

AMIAYA ENTERTAINMENT

P.O.BOX 1275

NEW YORK, NY 10159

tanianunez79@hotmail.com

No Regrets

ORDER FORM
Number of Copies

No Regrets	ISBN# 0-9745075-1-2	$14.95/Copy	_____
Flower's Bed	ISBN# 0-9745075-0-4	$14.95/Copy	_____

Mailing Options

PRIORITY POSTAGE (4-6 DAYS US MAIL): Add $4.95

Accepted form of Payments: Institutional Checks or Money Orders
(All Postal rates are subject to change.)

Please check with your local Post Office for change of rate and schedules.

Please Provide Us With Your Mailing Information:

Billing Address
Name: _____
Address: _____
Suite/Apartment#: _____
City: _____
Zip Code: _____

Shipping Address
Name: _____
Address: _____
Suite/Apartment#: _____
City: _____
Zip Code: _____

(Federal & State Prisoners, Please include your Inmate Registration Number)

Send Checks or Money Orders to:

AMIAYA ENTERTAINMENT
P.O.BOX 1275
NEW YORK, NY 10159
212-946-6565
www.amiayaentertainment.com

COMING SOON

COMING SOON
2005

Unwilling

to

Suffer

(infidelity is a muthaf^#k@)

Also by

Antoine "Inch" Thomas

www.amiayaentertainment.com

MelSoulTree...Melissa ROOTED in SOUL!!!

Some say she's an R& B Soul singer with a Gospel twist. Others say she is an R&B Soul Singer with a Jazzy twist. Yet everyone agrees she is MelSoulTree...Melissa ROOTED in SOUL!!! MelSoulTree's melodious voice and vocal range has been compared to the likes of Minnie Riperton, Phyllis Hyman, Chaka Kahn, Alicia Keys and Mariah Carey. In order to capture to the true essence of her voice you must experience her "live".

This talented vivacious beauty hails from NYC's borough of the Bronx. Born Melissa Antoinette Thomas she began to develop her love for music at the tender age of 4. She was exposed to different styles of music via the radio, her father (a poet & musician), her mother (a singer) and a musical family rooted in R&B Soul, Gospel, Jazz and Hip Hop music styles. MelSoulTree has been blanketed with music all her life. Despite all her influences she began studying to become an attorney. However, the call of music was so strong it dismissed that idea right away! By pursuing her love of music, her singing talents have taken her to places of which one could only dream. She has established herself as a gifted singer and songwriter. As an international artist she has toured extensively throughout Germany, France, Switzerland, Argentina, Uruguay, Chile, Canada and many areas of the U.S. as a featured soloist singing R&B, Jazz and Gospel music.

Some of MelSoulTree's many accomplishments include:
•   Graduating at the top of her Music class in the area of Jazz Vocal Music from the City College of New York under the direction of vocalist Sheila Jordan and bassist Ron Carter.

•   Recording for the Wild Pitch, Audio Quest and Select Record labels.
•   Former lead vocalist for the underground New York City based band Special Request.
•   Former lead singer and songwriter for the Lo-Key Records female group Legal Tender.
•   One of the youngest members to sing with the Duke Ellington Orchestra under the direction of Paul Ellington.
•   A frequent featured soloist for the Princeton Jazz Orchestra.
•   Although born long after the 60's era, she is currently one of the youngest singers touring with the world renowned Phil Spector's group "The

Crystals". She is known affectionately as "The Kid" by many of the veterans of the music business.

Can you believe most of these accomplishments where achieved as an unsigned artist? She is now establishing herself as one of the most sought after solo artists. Experience her for yourself during one of her live performances or again and again on CD. Don't miss the opportunity of witnessing the unique sound and vocal range of MelSoulTree...Melissa ROOTED in SOUL!!!

For CD, ticket and Booking information use one of the following contact methods:

On the WEB...visit the secure MelSoulTree Website:
www.soundclick.com/MelSoulTree

FOR MAIL ORDER FORMS & FAN CLUB INFORMATION...
MelSoulTree
P.O. Box 46
New York, NY 10475

The MelSoulTree 24 hour Hotline... (212) 560-7117

Coming this Fall...the long awaited album...MelSoulTree...Melissa ROOTED in SOUL!!!

MelSoulTree
212-560-7117

THEATRE

Production	Role	Producer(s)/Location
Just a Night Out	Marlena	The Negro Ensemble Co./The National Black Theatre
Black Theatre		
Killing Me Softly	Veronique	The Billie Holiday Theatre
The Harlem Nutcracker	Soloist/Chorus	The Brooklyn Academy of Music
In the Upper Room	Diane	Upper Room Productions
Ophelia's Cotillion	Gertrude	Rites & Reasons Theater/Brown University
A Way Out of No Way	Angel	Upper Room Productions
The Perfect Mate	Veronica	Positive Entertainment, N.E. Region
Primitive World	Naima	Nuyorican Cafe/National Black Theatre Festival
Raisin' Hell	Courtney	The Billie Holiday Theatre

CABARET/REVUE

The Duke Ellington Orchestra	Featured Soloist	Bird Land's
The Original Crystals (60's Girl Group)	Group Member	National
The Princeton Jazz Ensemble	Featured Soloist	Princeton University

INTERNATIONAL WORK

The Glory Gospel Singers	Soloist/Ensemble/Tour Manager	Germany Tour '02
The Glory Gospel Singers Tour '01	Soloist/Ensemble/Tour Manager	France & Geneva, Switzerland Tour '01
The Glory Gospel Singers	Soloist/Ensemble/Tour Manager	France Tour '00
The Inspirational Ensemble	Soloist/Choir	Argentina, Uruguay & Chile Tour '99
The Inspirational Ensemble	Soloist/Choir	Argentina & Uruguay Tour '98
The Talon Group	Soloist (Jazz/R&B)	Nice, St. Tropes & Monaco, France '98

AUDIO RECORDINGS

SONG TITLE	ARTIST(S)	ROLE	RECORD LABEL
Nobody	Legal Tender	Group Member	Lo Key Records
A Dream	Legal Tender	Group Member	Lo Key Records
Big & Tall	Chubb Rock	Featured Vocalist	Select Records
Walk A Little Closer	N-Tyce	Featured Vocalist	Wild Pitch Records
Bell y Cosima	Victor Lewis	Background Vocalist	Audio Quest Records
Lyrics 2 the Rhythm	Grand Master Flash/Essence	Featured Vocalist	Giant/Warner Records
The World Is Your	Two Positive	Featured Vocalist	2 Positive Records
The Beat Goes On	Two Positive	Featured Vocalist	2 Positive Records

EDUCATION/TRAINING

The Harlem Theatre Company	Actor Training
Haila Strauss	Dance Movement
The City College of New York	Vocal Performance/Music Education B.F.A
Harlem School of the Arts	College Preparatory Program/Vocal Scholarship
The Queen Broad casting School	D.J. Announcing and Speech

SPECIAL SKILLS

Solo, choral, choir, ensemble & background singing (gospel, jazz, & classical styles) in both live and studio recording capacities. Song writing, lead sheet transposition; Piano; Music Education and D. J. Announcing.

"I'm always willing to try and learn something new."

Updated 5/31/03